DO TEASE THE CHARMING BILLIONAIRE

Jewel Family Romance

CAMI CHECKETTS

COPYRIGHT

Do Tease the Charming Billionaire: Jewel Family Romance

Copyright © 2020 by Cami Checketts

All rights reserved.

No part of this book may be reproduced in any form or by any electronic or mechanical means, including information storage and retrieval systems, without written permission from the author, except for the use of brief quotations in a book review.

FREE BOOK

Sign up for Cami's VIP newsletter and receive a free ebook copy of *The Fearless Groom: Texas Titan Romance* by clicking here.

CHAPTER ONE

Rachel Jewel sauntered along the beach, savoring the feel of squishy sand between her toes and warm tropical air embracing her. She tilted her head up to the sun, not even caring that her strategically styled hair fell back away from her face, revealing scars she usually didn't let anyone besides immediate family view. Almost eight months ago an explosion had burned the left side of her cheek, jaw, neck, and the top of her shoulder. Enough time had passed, she should be ready to step up and conquer the world like she'd planned on, but she'd tried once after the accident and it had gone horribly. The experience had caused her to misplace her power, her moxie, her drive. They were going to reappear ... someday.

Spring had been coming to her parents' Vermont home where she'd mostly stayed since the accident, and she thought the beauty of earth's rebirth would invigorate her and help her reset her path. But no, nada, nothing. Apparently green shoots and flowers weren't enough to push past the humiliation of being blown up and disfigured by a psychotic jerk with a few sticks of dynamite.

The stimulus she hadn't planned on was her brother Luke appearing and begging her to come to this exotic private island he'd recently purchased and evaluate the customer service, the overall experience, and as a side note, see if the manager of the gorgeous resort was embezzling from him. Rachel didn't know if Luke really needed her "brilliant brain" like he claimed or if he was just trying to kick her out into the world, jump in the burning frying pan sort of thing. Her siblings and parents adored her and were naturally worried sick about her. Join the club. She agonized night and day about how to find Rachel Jewel again, and if she'd ever get brave enough to pursue her dreams of family law.

She'd surprised everyone, including herself, and said yes to Luke's proposal. She loved her family, but she not only yearned for some space, she absolutely needed to find her excitement for life again or she might die a pickled old woman. This island was a great spot to test the heat of the frying pan. With only a hundred guests and fifty employees it was low key and a beautiful paradise. It was five miles in circumference with a large palatial-looking main building set near the calm bay on the west side of the island. The main building housed a fancy restaurant, a buffet, game rooms, offices, a state-of-the-art spa and fitness facility, employee housing, and a massive swimming pool area with lots of landscaped gardens leading down to the beach near the bay where there was supposedly incredible snorkeling and scuba diving.

The guests each had their own bungalow through the trees stretching away from the main building. Some were smaller and stacked closer together in the wooded area near the main building. The farther away bungalows were larger with their own kitchens, their own private swimming pool, personal butler, and the beach only a dozen feet away. Rachel was in one of those suites. She could only imagine what it would cost to stay in one for a week. The island also boasted an adventure course, zipline, a waterfall near the eight-hundred-foot peak, and beautiful mountain biking and hiking trails through the jungle-like forest.

She approached the main building and the bay from the beach. She could hear people talking and children laughing and splashing in the swimming pool. She was careful around children, besides her niece Paisley and her new nephew Krew, afraid she might make other children uncomfortable or scared with her scarred face.

In August, shortly after the plastic surgeons had declared her mostly healed, she'd met with the Dean of Harvard's law school and three of the associate professors. She'd always dreamed of a career in family law and felt incredibly brave pursuing it, despite the scars disfiguring her face and neck. She'd felt the meeting went well and had almost convinced herself she could start school in the next couple of weeks. After the meeting, she'd been in the restroom and overheard two of the female professors talking about her. They thought her credentials, LSAT scores, and grades were more than sufficient, but they worried about her having a career in family law. In their minds, not only would judges and jury members be distracted or put off by her scars, they thought she would terrify and intimidate little children, who would be her most important clients and were already going through hard things with their families. She could still hear the one professor's voice, "Children who are struggling shouldn't have to also have nightmares about their lawyer's disfigured face." The words hadn't been said snidely, simply matter of fact, which made it even harder to take.

Rachel had waited until they left the restroom to sneak out. She'd made it home to her bedroom before she broke down. She'd hoped in this modern age of acceptance her scars wouldn't affect her career, but she didn't want to scare anyone, especially children. After that, she styled her hair in front of her face and neck whenever she went in public but mostly she stuck close to her family and had spent the entire fall, winter, and early spring in Vermont.

A yacht was sailing into the bay and she found herself stopping in the sand to watch its approach. It was gorgeous—bright white with sleek lines. Whoever owned that piece of beautiful metal wouldn't blink an eye at the cost of staying at this exotic island retreat.

About a dozen people walked off the yacht and Rachel noticed that at least one staff member fawned over each new guest, taking their bags and welcoming them. She also saw Preston Sant, the manager she was supposed to be "watching", was right there in a suit and tie beaming as he welcomed the group. Preston had done the same when Rachel arrived from nearby Belize earlier this morning in the helicopter used by the resort to shuttle guests to the island. She hadn't been particularly impressed or put off by Preston as he gave her a tour. He was a little smooth for her, something definitely was hiding behind his practiced smile and pretty-boy perfection. Who wore a suit in eighty degrees with eighty percent humidity? Yet she couldn't fault him for that. He was putting on a professional vibe for the high-dollar crowd that could afford the island retreat.

She watched closer as the last man exited the yacht, turned back to say something to the captain and then was pounced upon by Preston. Rachel couldn't hear their conversation and she couldn't see the other man's face from this angle, but she was intrigued by his broad, tall frame. He had wide shoulders, a tapered waist, and muscular calves all nicely displayed in a fitted cotton shirt and golf shorts. The man's confidence, and the way Preston was simpering over him, revealed he was wealthy and powerful. Rachel had no problem with wealthy, well-built guys, but she simply wasn't in the market for any man, not until she came to terms with her deformed face, her resentment toward the man who hurt her, and her altered future plans.

She tucked her long hair around the left side of her face and neck. With the help of hair extensions to make her fire-damaged dark locks thicker and longer, she was pretty certain no one could see anything but a small glimpse of the scars on her cheek through her sheet of dark hair. Though the scars had gotten less noticeable over the past eight months, the deformity wasn't going anywhere.

She decided she'd turn around and walk back to her bungalow rather than go enjoy the spa right now. She used to be a social bug but now she defensively leaned toward peace and quiet. The new people who'd just arrived weren't exactly a quiet crowd.

As she started to turn, the man she'd been watching also pivoted with Preston to start walking up the docks for his welcome tour of the impressive island and facilities. She'd received the VIP tour this morning and had been very impressed with Luke's new purchase, excited to spend a week in paradise. This island took all-inclusive to a new level. No upcharges on anything, including the spa, scuba diving, ziplining, the adventure course, mountain bikes, specialty drinks, room service, and more. Everything you wanted was right there, handed over with a smile; and tips were all included as well. If the customer wanted, they could leave an extra tip in an envelope at the end of the week for employees who were very impressive to them, but there was no need to carry your wallet or even a key card around as the bungalow doors were re-programmed to a numbered code of the guest's choice each week.

The man's gaze swept the main building and expansive pool area, and then rotated to the beach where she stood fifty yards away. Their eyes locked and held, and she sucked in a breath, shocked by the impact those deep brown eyes had on her, even from a distance. She could see his face clearly, and it was as impressive and intriguing as his fit body. He was definitely a handsome man with a straight nose, high brow, strong jaw, and a cleft in his chin that she really liked, but it was the power and allure of his dark-brown eyes framed with thick lashes and dark eyebrows that really pulled her in.

She found herself giving him a challenging smile in return and throwing her hair back over her shoulder, tossing her head in a flirtatious gesture that she'd mastered in college. She realized her mistake quickly and sucked in a breath as if someone had punched her. What had she just done?

It was too late, he'd seen her, all of her. His gaze changed from welcoming to surprised, or maybe shocked would be a better word, but it wasn't the shock that reverberated through her, it was the compassion. His eyes quickly swept over the mottled, patched, bumpy, disgusting skin of her left cheek, chin, and neck then refocused on her eyes as he gave her a welcoming, appealing smile.

Horrified, Rachel yanked her hair forward to cover the scars again, pivoted, and strode away through the thick sand. The luxurious feel of the sand earlier had now morphed into a trap that was dragging her down and halting her progress. She wanted to run from that handsome man and the fact that he'd seen her scars. Would he have nightmares like the law professor had said children would? Could she avoid him over the next week and still do the job Luke had asked of her? She doubted it, and her stomach squirmed with anxiety.

The old, feisty, funny, confident Rachel would be telling the new Rachel that she was acting like a complete wuss. Yes, he'd looked at the scars, who wouldn't, but he'd moved past them and still smiled so becomingly at her. Maybe not everyone would be repulsed by her like she feared. Former Rachel would say she should be heading the other direction and introducing herself to the man.

She shoved former Rachel face-first into the sand and angled up the beach to the walking path that would lead her to her secluded bungalow and safety, for the moment. Why had she let Luke talk her into this and not begged Eve and Paisley to come with her? Why had she thought she was ready to reenter society? Not that a secluded island retreat was anything like her old social life, but it was still too much for the social wart she had become.

Pounding footsteps rang from the palm tree lined path to the south, vibrating through her like a gong banging repeatedly. She stopped short. She glanced that direction and saw the very man she'd strode away from running her direction.

Rachel froze. She didn't know how to skirt around him and get to her bungalow without encountering him and she refused to spin and go the other direction and make it obvious she was avoiding him. The way his gaze was trained on her as he ran told her his very intent was to run into her.

He slowed his steps as he approached, leaving the firmer

path through the trees and making his way down the beach toward her. He had a welcoming smile on his handsome face but something kind and understanding in his dark eyes revealed that he knew the truth---she'd run because of the scars.

Rachel may have become an expert at avoiding people, and especially confident, impressive men, the past eight months, but she wasn't as far removed from her former self as she'd feared. She stood straight and tilted her chin imperiously, tucking her hair into place so he didn't get assaulted with another view of her grisly skin. She wished she didn't care. She kept telling herself she didn't. She'd gone to numerous therapists and claimed she'd come to terms with the scarring and assuring them that she'd never been defined by the beauty of her face anyway. The fact that she kept pulling her long hair in front of her face to try and hide the scars said she definitely did care. She'd never told anyone about that woman's voice echoing in her head, "Children who are struggling shouldn't have to also have nightmares about their lawyer's disfigured face."

"Rachel Jewel?" He kept coming toward her with that large smile and now his hand was extended.

Rachel didn't advance toward him, instead she held her ground, at least she could be proud of herself for that. She smiled and extended her own hand. "Yes. How'd you know?"

Their hands met and suddenly Rachel didn't care how he knew her name, didn't care if he'd Googled her and read every lame post someone had made about the former "perfect" model being disfigured.

His large palm pressed against her smaller one and then his fingers wrapped around the back of her hand and he held on. His touch was magnetic and somehow lifted her spirits. She felt like she could handle anything if their hands were joined.

"Um ..." His confident smile slipped as he looked down at their hands then back up at her. Had he felt the connection as well? "Preston told me who you are. We both knew your brother Caleb in college, well we played lacrosse against him. He was at Duke .... As you know," he gave her a chagrined smile, "and Preston and I played for Syracuse. Caleb was only a freshman when we were seniors but he was already an incredible athlete. His footwork and stick skills were better than anyone I'd played against. He destroyed us almost single-handedly ..." He faded off, shook his head, pulled his hand back, and pushed it through his dark hair. "Sorry, I'm rambling."

She smiled, liking that this obviously successful, handsome man was rambling. Was he affected by touching her hand like she had been with him or was he rambling to cover his embarrassment because he'd seen her scars? That tampered her smile.

"The Jewel family shows no mercy when it comes to sports," she said.

He chuckled and nodded. "I saw that firsthand."

She smiled. So, he'd gone to college with Preston and they'd both played against Caleb. Were he and Preston still close? Could this provide the insight she needed into whether Preston was running the island to the best of his ability or skimming employee paycheck funds like Luke suspected? She realized the ultra-appealing, dark-eyed man standing in front of her hadn't told her his name in all his rambling. "And you are?" she asked.

"Oh, sorry." He shook his head. "Abe, Abe Bradford."

He put out his hand as if to shake again. Rachel glanced down at his hand and couldn't help laughing. She'd forgotten how fun it was to not only banter with handsome men but know because of her brilliance, beauty, and funny personality she made them stumble over their feet or their words. That surprised her.

She hadn't felt that since the explosion and had feared the old Rachel was buried too deep.

He also looked down at his hand then back up at her and let it fall to his side. "I guess we already did that." He laughed along with her. "I'm a little off my game today."

Rachel liked that he would admit that. She tilted her head back toward his yacht, at least she assumed it was his yacht. "Traveling will do that to you."

His dark gaze gave her another compliment as it slowly swept over her face. "I don't know that we can blame traveling."

She smiled. "Where did you sail from?"

"I keep my yacht in Cancun." His eyes widened as if he hadn't been ready to admit to her it was his yacht.

She nodded. Pivoting slightly, she walked to the path that led through the thick trees and to the bungalows, ready to be out of the sun. He fell into step beside her, thankfully on her right side.

"And you flew there from ...?" She snuck a glance at him, not sure why she was being so nosy but he was intriguing, and even though he'd seen her scars his eyes weren't flickering to the spot where they hid, and he wasn't acting like they bothered him. Impressive man, or a good actor? She wasn't sure yet.

"Buffalo. My company is based out of Buffalo, New York."

"What company do you own?"

"Bradford International."

She laughed. "Oh, of course. Did you oh-so-humbly name it after yourself or was that your dad or granddad?"

He smiled, not seeming the least bit offended by her slight jab to his pride. "It was me. I started it myself. Figured nobody would know what it is we do with just my name on the business license, and the international in the title makes it seem like we're more impressive than we actually are." He winked.

She liked that he was trying for humility, but they must do something very impressive if he owned his own yacht and could bring a group on a vacation here. "So, you probably can't tell me what you do, or you might have to silence me?" She stopped as they reached the pool deck outside her bungalow and she turned to face him again. Here in the shade it was even nicer to stare into his handsome face.

"I would hate to have to silence you," he murmured, his gaze warm and seductive as if he thought she was exquisitely beautiful. She used to get those looks many times a day. Had they stopped because of her scars or because she'd shut herself away? She pushed all the worries away. Flirting with a handsome man was no time to be self-analyzing.

"I'm not easily silenced." She raised a challenging eyebrow.

He chuckled. "I'll bet. My company sells home security systems."

She liked that he hadn't made her pull it out of him. "Wait. You aren't those annoying college students who knock on the door all the time, ignoring no soliciting signs to try to peddle security systems?"

He grinned. "Yes, ma'am, we are, except ignoring the no soliciting sign part. Selling those systems got me through college, then after some ... detours, I was able to start my own company and it took off."

Though she couldn't see it anymore, her eyes darted through the trees to where his yacht rested. "It looks like it took off." She studied him for a few seconds then said, "So, young entrepreneur, quick success story, eh?"

He gave her a definite smirk and said, "I've been out of college for ten years, not sure how quick of a success story that is."

"Whoa. I wouldn't have guessed. So you're about ... thirty-two?"

"Thirty-one. Started college at seventeen."

She stared at his handsome face. "You look pretty good for an old man."

He chuckled. "And how old are you, Miss Jewel, if you don't mind me asking?"

"Twenty-four." Twenty-five in a month but she didn't need to shorten the age gap between them. It might be a buffer that she could use.

His eyes swept over her and he grinned. "You look pretty good for a young lady."

She smiled but backed toward her door. "It was nice to meet you."

He stepped forward, his dark eyes suddenly intense, giving her an indicator of one of the factors that had helped him achieved success—he didn't take no for an answer. "Have dinner with me ... please."

The please was an afterthought to soften the demand of his request. She shouldn't have liked his presumptuous tone and the intensity of his gaze but she'd always admired confident men, wanted a man who could stand by her side not mooch off her or her family's success. Before her accident she'd known she would take the world by storm. Now she wasn't so sure.

She surprised herself by wanting to spend more time with him. She wanted it badly. She swallowed and admitted, "I agreed to dine with Preston tonight."

He paused for a beat, his eyes and mouth tightened, and then he nodded. "Smart move by my friend."

"Nice to have met you," she repeated then hurried across the deck, typed in the code for the door, and slid in, only letting herself look back once. He was focused on her and when he caught her eye, he gave her one more slow, sexy grin.

Rachel hesitantly returned the smile then let the door close behind her. She rested back against it and sighed dreamily. He was ... incredible and she was definitely, definitely not in the market for a wealthy, fabulous man to date. Yet, the entire interaction had left her elated and wondering if she'd misjudged how men would respond to her scars or if Abe Bradford was impressive in more areas than success and good looks.

CHAPTER TWO

Abe slowly backed away from Rachel's bungalow, smiling to himself. She was ... incredible. Too bad he was here for a company retreat and not to flirt with a gorgeous and intriguing woman. When she'd given him a flirtatious gaze and flipped her hair away from her face back on the beach, he'd received a brief glimpse of the mottled skin on the left side of her face and neck. When she'd quickly pulled her hair back and spun away, he'd only had one purpose: get to her fast and make sure she knew she was gorgeous and shouldn't hide the scars.

Walking back toward the main area he thought how he'd wimped out. He hadn't told her how attractive she was, how the scars added to her appeal, gave her character, and showed she had been through hard things, in his mind the complete picture made her even more beautiful. He wished he'd spilled all of that, but he had at least enjoyed flirting with her.

He remembered when he'd heard about Caleb Jewel's sister being burned from an explosion last year and had felt bad for the woman and thought she looked beautiful but sad in the pictures. Seeing her face to face, and then holding her hand in his, had absolutely floored him.

Abe knew himself. He was determined, driven, and when he saw something he wanted, he didn't hesitate to go after it. Prison had taught him to seize the moment, and to not trust anyone. Could he seize some moments with the beautiful Rachel Jewel this week? For some reason, he thought she might have more trust issues than he did, or maybe with her injury being recent she was simply learning how to deal with her face being burned and people's reactions to it.

"Well, that was interesting," Preston drawled out as he met Abe on one of the paths that led to the main building.

"Sorry, did I ditch you?" Abe grinned at him.

"Ran away mid-sentence," Preston said back. "She's fabulous, isn't she?"

"Yes, sir." Abe gave him a quick glance. "Are you ...?"

"No," Preston inserted quickly, touching his perfect hair, his deep-blue eyes glinting. "I suspect she's here on her brother's orders. Not exactly the woman I should be cozying up to, no matter how beautiful she is."

"Caleb?" Abe was confused.

"No, her brother Luke recently bought this property." Preston's smile was forced. "And immediately sent a spy to see if I'm up to snuff."

Abe shook his head. "I think you're worrying about nothing. She's been through something horrific and her brother probably sent her here for some rest and recoup. Besides." He gestured to the open-air main area with polished teakwood floors, water features, and flower arrangements abounding. Smiling staff awaited their approach to the front desk, offering Abe a strawberry daquiri. "Look at this place. You're doing amazing and booked out what ... a year in advance?"

"Usually." Preston puffed his chest out. "Thanks, man. It's great to have you and your people here. It's great to see you."

"You as well."

He and Preston had met their junior year of high school traveling together with a national lacrosse team and gotten close being roommates and playing college lacrosse together. Their senior year of college they'd both fallen in love with the beauty Angel Falslev. Abe swallowed down the bile of revulsion. The very name could still make his gut tighten with anger. Over ten years ago she'd chosen Abe. He couldn't think how many times he'd wished she hadn't. Especially when she'd framed him and he'd spent three months in a prison cell. Preston had remained a true friend throughout the years, even when Abe was convicted.

Preston informed him that Abe's employees were all on introductory tours or settled into their bungalows and then took him around the impressive property and beautiful island in a golf cart. By the time they arrived at the impressive two-story bungalow Abe would stay in for the week it was close to dinnertime. He thanked his friend, showered off the humidity, wondering how in the world Preston handled a suit in this heat. Being from upstate New York, this tropical weather in March was almost too hot for Abe. He dressed in a short-sleeved off-white chambray shirt and fitted gray golf pants. He wasn't a very good golfer, not enough patience, but he loved the pants and shorts for comfort and especially in the hot weather they looked good, didn't wrinkle, and were breathable.

As he walked into the fancy dining room, he saw his group of employees already seated at a large round table off to the right. He raised a hand and started that way but heard movement behind him. Turning, he saw a vision in red and swayed on his feet.

Rachel stood right behind him wearing a long formal dress. Her dark eyes were outlined with smoky makeup and her lips were a deep red that matched the dress. She gave him a welcoming smile and he let himself appreciate the entire exotic effect of her appearance for a minute. The dress was floor length but had a slit on one leg that came well above her knee and showed off enough beautiful tanned leg to make his mouth go dry. Her right shoulder was bare and the dress tucked around her chest on that side. On the left side it covered her shoulder with a capped sleeve but most of the left side of the silky red bodice was covered with her long, dark hair that swooped from her forehead across her cheek and then was pulled forward to cover her neck and chin on the left side. He wished he could help her know she didn't need to cover up, but he could at least tell her how beautiful she was.

"Rachel," he breathed out, automatically extending his hand. "You are exquisite."

She put her hand in his, and just like this afternoon, he was struck by the power that seemed to surge through him at her very feminine touch. He could be her Tarzan or Superman or whoever she wanted him to be when she had her hand in his. He wanted to be more for her. A billionaire from upstate New York who had scrapped his future out of nothing but sheer will and his own two hands wasn't nearly good enough for a woman with such light, intelligence, and grit.

Acting like a sappy charmer, well, like Preston really, he bent low and brought her hand up to his lips. "Beautiful," he said, then remembered that he'd already said she was exquisite. What was he doing? He wasn't here to fall for a woman. In fact, falling for a woman hadn't been on his radar since Angel backstabbed and betrayed him almost ten years ago.

"Thank you." Rachel gifted him with a smile that made her even more appealing. "I didn't figure you for a 'compliments flowing like honey from his tongue' kind of guy."

He laughed and tilted closer to her. "Would you believe me if I told you that I'm usually not?"

"No."

Oh, he liked her sass. Most women were enamored with his success and his looks and either flirted brazenly with him or acted like he was Zeus. Rachel did neither, but at least she did seem interested in him. He caught a glimpse of Preston coming their way and remembered Rachel was supposed to dine with his lifelong friend. He cursed and she lifted an eyebrow.

"Sorry," he muttered. He'd picked up some habits in prison his mom didn't like and swearing was one of them. He lowered his voice as Preston came closer. "Meet me on the beach after dinner?"

Rachel scrunched her nose and tilted her head to the left, her long hair trailing almost to the curve of her waist. "We'll see."

"Rachel. Abe." Preston greeted them each warmly then said, "You'll have to excuse us, my friend, this lovely lady and I have a dinner appointment."

Rachel glanced back at him and Abe tried to smooth the glower pulling his brow and his lips tight. Preston had claimed he wasn't interested in Rachel. Was that true? Maybe his friend was just trying to butter up the boss's sister, but as Preston walked away with his hand on Rachel's lower back, lower than Abe thought it should be, he didn't think his friend's intentions were as clear or pure as they should be.

He straightened his shoulders and headed to his table. It wasn't fair to the associates who'd earned this incredible getaway to have to deal with a moody boss, but when he heard Rachel laugh throatily at something Preston said, he thought this dinner might be worse torture than serving time for the woman who'd betrayed him.

Though Preston was charming, funny, handsome, and attentive, Rachel couldn't keep her eyes from straying to Abe throughout dinner. He'd said she was exquisite and beautiful. Though she'd teased him about it, he truly didn't seem like the type to throw around empty compliments. Could he be sincere and believe she was exquisite and beautiful? She could easily say the same about him. There was something about him that just appealed to her, far above any of the men she'd dated before her accident. Powerful, confident, handsome, all those described Abe, but it was something else. He'd been through something that had changed him from steel to titanium. She wanted to get to know him, find out about the detours in his life.

Maybe he'd lost someone close to him, that might be it, that depth of character, yet pain in his eyes. It reminded her of Isaac. Her brother had done and seen things in the military that had changed him, and she thought Abe shared that same almost haunted look sometimes. Maybe he'd been burned by someone he loved or, she thought bitterly, burned in an explosion. She pulled her hair tighter around her neck, hoping Abe hadn't been through pain like she'd known. She'd been knocked out initially and then kept heavily sedated, but the recovery had been horrific.

"Is it Abe that's got you so distracted?" Preston asked from far too close.

Rachel whirled and then leaned back against the padded chair, eating a bite of salmon and giving Preston time to move back into his own space before she answered. He kept looking at her as if waiting for her answer meant everything to him. He was great with people and attentive, which she thought were important qualities for a manager, but she didn't need him to be quite so attentive to her.

Rachel dabbed her mouth with her napkin. "He's an interesting man."

"That he is." There was a hint of something in Preston's gaze that made her uneasy, but then it was gone and his deep-blue eyes was full of easy humor again.

"You've been friends a long time?" she asked.

"Oh yeah. Met on a national FCA lacrosse team our junior year of high school and then ended up roommates and teammates at Syracuse."

"FCA?"

"Fellowship of the Christian Athletes."

So, Abe was a Christian. She liked that, but what was that underlying hardness and grit about? He wore it like a second skin. "Did he serve in the military?" she asked abruptly.

"No." Preston's gaze was intent on her. "Why would you ask that?"

She took a sip of her water and shrugged. "I don't know. Just trying to get a bead on him. There's something in his eyes …" She trailed off, realizing nothing could come of her obsessing over a man. Her first entry into life or society or whatever you wanted to call it since the accident, she definitely didn't need to be rushing to date the second man she'd seen. He'd asked her to go on a walk on the beach. *Maybe I will take him up on that.* A smile played on her lips at the thought.

"He's the dark, mysterious type, right?" Preston smiled easily and lifted his wine glass as if saluting her. "Maybe you'll get through to him ... no other woman has been able to since ..."

Rachel's heart thumped a little faster. She risked a glance at Abe. He was focused her way. When he caught her gaze, he lifted his chin and gave her a secretive smile then refocused on the conversation at his table. What had happened to him? The puzzle of it was enough to make her forget her own troubles and insecurities, which she liked almost as much as she liked flirting with him.

"Since?"

Preston shook his head. "Sorry. Please forget I said anything. So, what do you think of your brother's investment so far?" He spread his arms to indicate the fancy dining room but she knew he meant the entire island.

"It's singularly impressive. The perfect vacation retreat in my mind. Luke will be thrilled with how well-kept everything is and how fabulously the staff treats the guests."

"Thank you." Preston bowed his head slightly as if he deserved all the praise for the lush island retreat.

"I especially like how the guests don't even need to carry a key card or wallet as everything is included." Since most of her clothing didn't have pockets and she loved leaving her cell phone in the room and being disconnected, it was wonderful to not be hiding a keycard or money in her bra.

"I think a lot of guests like that, and who could complain about drinking daquiris until you're sick or spending an entire day in a state-of-the-art spa if you want to?"

"Good point, or if you're a teenager all the ziplines, adventure course, or scuba diving you can take?" She looked squarely at him and asked, "Do the staff complain about not getting extra tips?"

His mouth and eyes tightened but he shook his head easily. "They're well compensated and the guests often leave generous tips at the end of their week's stay."

Rachel studied him. He was hiding something, but what? Luke thought Preston might be skimming from the employee funds, but he didn't know. The former owner had trusted Preston implicitly and bragged about how smart and competent he was. Preston did payroll and minor accounting because the resort wasn't that large. Luke and his wife, Mar, had given a couple of friends a week at the resort shortly after they bought it in January. Their friends had overheard some employees complaining that the pay was lower than they'd originally been promised and the tips weren't always enough to make up for the lack. The employees left their families for six to nine months then returned home for six to eight weeks, depending on their job and status with the company, similar to a cruise ship. Luke wanted to make sure they were well-compensated so he would not only be good to his people but have faithful, happy employees who pampered his high-dollar clients like they would expect at a unique and impressive resort such as this.

"Do you think Luke and his lovely wife will come stay soon?" Preston asked as the waiter took their dinner plates and immediately served Rachel's cheesecake and Preston's tiramisu.

"I don't know." Rachel replied stiffly as she took a bite of cheesecake. The cake was creamy, rich, and delectable and the thinly sliced ripe mango, passionfruit, and pineapple were sweet with a creamy coconut sauce that seemed to melt on her tongue.

She forgot about her quest to figure out what Preston was up to, and even to sneak glances at Abe, as she savored every bite.

Preston smiled secretively at her as she put her fork down and declared, "That was the most delicious thing I've ever eaten."

"I'll know what to bring if I ever need to bribe you."

She should've laughed. She thought he'd said it as a tease, but there was something instantly uncomfortable about him saying he would need to bribe her. You didn't care to bribe somebody unless you had something to hide.

At least enough time had passed that she felt she could thank him for the pleasant conversation and excuse herself. As she walked out of the restaurant, she felt eyes on her. She glanced over and saw Abe staring at her. "Beach?" he mouthed.

She smiled and nodded, unable to resist the chance to meet up with him again. Their last conversation was far too short. As she strode from the restaurant, she realized she wasn't even worrying if her hair was in place. Abe had glimpsed her scars the first time he saw her, and he didn't seem bothered by them at all. In fact, he seemed as interested in her as the many men who flocked to her before the accident. It made her wonder: were those female professors at Harvard right and she was going to terrify people, especially children, or were her brothers and Eve right and the scars didn't make her repulsive? The real question was—was Abe an anomaly, something special, or could there be others who would react so kindly to her scars?

CHAPTER THREE

Rachel hurried to her room and changed out of her formal dress. Maybe she should've stayed in it but she wanted to enjoy the time spent with Abe on the beach, not feel poured into her custom-made formal gown. She put on a comfortable white sundress, pulled her hair over her left shoulder and frowned. Pushing it back she looked at the scarring, the bumpy, discolored skin. The only good thing she could see about it was it was only on the bottom of her cheek, her chin, the side of her neck, and the very top of her shoulder. The scarring was easily covered, but she was already getting sick of covering it. She'd never been a girl that hid in the shadows and she hated what that explosion and Flint Brooks had taken from her.

Now was not the time to psychoanalyze herself or decide to throw caution to the wind and put her hair in a messy bun. Pulling her hair back in place over the scars, she hurried to blot the shine from her nose and apply some cinnamint lip gloss. Her makeup was a little heavy for a stroll on the beach, but she wasn't going to waste time taking it off.

She didn't put on shoes as she slid out of the bungalow. Abe hadn't said what part of the beach to meet on, but he knew where her room was so she decided to head straight out to the beach past her private pool. Her pool glowed blue in the night and a half moon graciously sent light from above through the thick trees.

She threaded through one of the paths in the trees back toward the main building. Suddenly, she heard voices coming her way. Rachel slid behind a palm tree. Partially because she didn't want to get hung up talking to anyone and delay being with Abe and partially because she hadn't forgotten her mission of finding out if Preston was hiding anything from his employer, her brother. So far, the employees had all been smiling beacons of happy service and hadn't responded to her fishing. She might have to be a bit sneakier and overhear some conversations like Luke and Mar's friends had.

She recognized Preston's voice and caught a glimpse of his handsome profile. Goldmine. She couldn't place the blonde who was with him. It was too dim to see her face clearly but she was definitely not an employee in that fancy dress. A guest? Preston's lover?

The woman stopped on the path and turned to Preston. "I had to eat alone in my room. *Why* are you shutting me away?"

Definitely the lover. And he was hiding her away? Interesting.

"Because, my angel love," Preston's voice was soft and conciliatory, as if he were explaining something to a young, frightened child. "You've burned through most of the money we ... procured and now I need to trick him again so we can get more."

Oh, my, definite goldmine. Preston had "procured" money before? He was an embezzler. This woman was his accomplice? Rachel tried to see the face of the woman Preston called his love, but she was turned away from her and in the shadows.

The woman pushed out her hip and tossed her long hair. "Trick him, steal from him, what do I care? Just get us the money. Ugh! I hate hiding out. I hate that he's still controlling my life." She folded her arms under her very generous bosom and harrumphed. Rachel felt like she was watching a soap opera, with even worse than normal acting. Who were they talking about? Luke? But Luke wasn't here. Rachel didn't know that this lover's quarrel, if it could be called that, as Preston pandered to this woman worse than he did to the guests, had anything to do with Luke. Maybe Preston wasn't embezzling from his boss but from someone else?

"I know, I know, love," he said all placating and phony. "But if he sees you, he might try and have you arrested."

Arrested? This just got deeper and uglier.

"Ha! He'd be putty in my hands in seconds, just like he always was, just like you are every day." She grabbed Preston's suit coat and yanked him in. Preston didn't resist and soon the sounds of embarrassing slurping noises had Rachel wanting to dry heave. She thought she would be safe to slip away and tiptoed toward the beach. Rather than their conversation being a piece to the embezzlement puzzle it was an entirely new puzzle to solve. She didn't mind. She liked the challenge. It sounded like Preston was involved with a woman he was keeping hidden to protect her from being arrested if somebody saw her. Who could they be hiding from? She didn't think it had anything to do with Luke or his worries of embezzlement, but it was intriguing. If only she could've seen the woman's face or, even better, gotten a name.

As soon as she couldn't hear them any longer she headed straight for the water, walking in the moist sand with an occasional soft, warm wave breaking over her feet. Tomorrow she promised herself she'd pretend she was her brave former self and swim in the ocean, go snorkeling, go do the adventure course, the ziplines, hike and bike. It didn't matter if she did it all alone and it didn't matter if her scars showed. That was another bonus to this amazing island, anonymity. If a celebrity wanted, they could book the entire resort and never worry about paparazzi snapping pictures of them not sucking their gut in for two seconds.

After seeing Preston and his woman, she'd changed course and walked away from the main part of the resort. She couldn't glimpse any more lights through the trees from the bungalows. Where was Abe? What if he stood her up? She flinched at the thought. She'd never been stood up before. Men had crawled over each other trying to get her attention. Before ... She put a hand underneath her hair to her scars, hating the feel of the bumpy skin and trying to tell herself for the hundredth time that it didn't matter, couldn't affect her. Sadly, she hadn't bought the lies yet.

"Rachel!"

The call came from behind her. Abe. She whipped around to face him. A soft breeze lifted her hair. She tucked her hair in tighter and walked back toward him.

Abe jogged up to her, a grin on his handsome face. He stopped in front of her. "Hey."

"Hey yourself." Rachel returned his smile and then tilted her head. "You want to explore the beach in this direction?"

"I'd love to."

They fell into step together in the soft sand, neither saying anything as they walked along the beach, the lights and sounds of the resort disappearing behind them. Rachel had a brief thought that she shouldn't be walking into the dark with a man she barely knew, but there was just something peaceful and reassuring about Abe. She couldn't imagine he'd ever done anything unsavory, or would, especially not with her. Preston had alluded at dinner to something happening to Abe, but she knew it wouldn't be anything he'd done wrong. Maybe he'd lost someone close to him and that had given him the depth she'd seen in his eyes. Maybe some idiotic woman had broken his heart. She snuck a glance at him. Nah. No woman would be that dumb.

"How was dinner?" Abe broke the silence.

"Delicious, but some handsome guy kept distracting me. How was yours?"

"The same."

"Some handsome guy kept distracting you?" She couldn't hide the smile in her voice.

He chuckled. "It was a beautiful lady." He reached out and took her hand. A pulse of warmth and desire swept through her. "Exquisitely beautiful." He squeezed her hand.

Rachel grinned. They walked hand in hand and she felt like the accident had never happened. With her hand in Abe's she was complete, whole, and confident.

"Tell me more about you," she requested.

"Nothing too exciting to tell. Two great parents, one annoying sister."

"Nah, don't do that. Sisters are the best. Just ask my brothers."

He laughed. "Okay, you're right. My little sister is the best. Allison simply likes to annoy me."

"What does she do to annoy you?"

"Tells me nonstop I should, 'find a worthy chick and make babies'."

Rachel chortled. "Wow. That sounds like something a mom would say not a sister. Well, except for the 'chick' part."

"Right? Honestly, she's great. She just wants me to take the pressure off her 'finding a worthy dude and making babies'." He glanced her way with a grin. Even in the dim light from the half-moon she thought he was the most attractive man she'd ever seen, and that was saying something because she'd dated a lot of handsome men. Too bad she wasn't in the market to be a worthy chick and make babies with him.

"What does Allison do? Besides annoy you and avoid marriage?"

"She's an actress. No huge roles yet but she's done well with the supporting roles she's won."

"Good for her."

"Yeah. We're proud of her. My parents go to California regularly to visit her. Plus, it's not a bad deal to get out of Rochester in the wintertime."

"You grew up in Rochester?"

"Yes, ma'am."

"Grew up in Rochester, college in Syracuse, now your company is based in Buffalo. You just have an affinity for upstate New York?"

"For sure. Plus, I'm a huge Buffalo Bills fan."

"Aha. That makes sense. Broncos for me. Always has been."

"Really? Even after that Broncos player tried to frame Caleb for murder last month?"

They came upon a rocky outcropping on the beach. If it had been daylight she would've tried to go around it but as it was, they both turned and started back the other way. Caleb had been framed, in a really weird way. The guy was Caleb's fiancée's ex-husband and had known he was dying from numerous head injuries sustained from football, so he framed Caleb for his death. So sad and disturbing.

"Yeah that was nuts, but you can't judge an entire team off one crazy train."

"Hmm." His thumb gently stroked across the back of her hand and made her thoughts scatter and her hand tingle. "I don't know. Any excuse to bag on the Broncos."

"Oh!" She gasped and probably should've pulled her hand free, but she didn't want to. She chose to push at his shoulder with her free hand instead. "I thought you were lobbying for more time spent with me, but you've just risked me never speaking to you again."

He chuckled. "Forgive me. I am definitely lobbying for more time spent with you. I'll forget my lifelong allegiance to the Bills."

She flushed with pleasure. He did want more time with her. How to respond? "We'll see," she said evasively. "The island isn't big enough to escape you so maybe I'll have to give you that time."

He rubbed her hand with his thumb again. "I've never felt so lucky."

Neither of them said anything for a few minutes and the lights of the bungalows and resort glowed up ahead. She could've walked with her hand in Abe's all night.

"So are you in college or working or ..."

"I just graduated with my MBA." Just? It would be a year in May. She really needed to decide what to do with her degree if she didn't pursue her dreams of going on to law school. She'd receive a five-million-dollar inheritance on her birthday next month. Should she start a business like some of her brothers were pushing her to? She'd always felt like family law would be her spot, especially since getting to know Caleb's fiancée, Emily, and her adorable son, Krew. In Rachel's opinion, they'd needed better protection from Emily's ex and more help from their lawyer. Rachel felt as if family law was something that could challenge her, while allowing her to give back by protecting innocent parents and children. But the question always lingered in her mind, were those professors right and she would only terrify the children? That made her sick inside and was the last thing she wanted to do.

"Congrats," he said. "What are your plans now?"

Why did his question feel almost … contrived? Was she too sensitive or did he know too much? He'd seen her scars earlier today when she'd unconsciously tossed her hair. How to test him?

She stopped on the sand, knowing her bungalow was a short distance away. It was still quiet, but she could hear laughter and music coming from the main building.

"You know what happened with Caleb, his fiancée Emily, and the Broncos player, obviously you saw that online," she stated quietly. "Did you see anything about me?"

His mouth pursed and his eyes seemed to darken with concern. The answer he chose to give would decide a lot about their future together and he seemed to sense the significance of the question.

"I did," he admitted. "I was very sorry to hear about your accident. Are you recovering all right?"

She looked out at the soft Caribbean waves rolling onto the sand. "All right" was a matter of perspective. For someone with less aspirations and confidence from a family who weren't a bunch of superstars she would probably be viewed as doing spectacular. For her, for being a Jewel, she was a pathetic mess. A waste of space in her mind. She'd tried to put herself out there with the Harvard Law interview and the women's comments and concerns in that restroom had knocked her back down, hard. She needed to try again, but she was scared. It all made her mad at herself and furious at Flint Brooks, the man who had set the explosion.

"Forgive me," Abe said softly, stepping in closer to her. "I didn't mean to pry."

Rachel prayed for some of the sass she used to possess. She looked straight in his eyes and said, "No apology necessary. I am doing just fabulous. It would take more than a little explosion and some third-degree burns to take me down."

His eyes widened slightly with surprise but then glowed with appreciation. It was good to know she could still fake confidence and even an impressive man like Abe would be snow jobbed by her.

"You are ... so impressive to me." Abe's voice got low and husky and his gaze swept over her with approval and desire.

Rachel finally felt like she was the confident woman she'd always been and now was trying hard to portray. Her mom had been a big proponent of "fake it till you make it," whether teaching them to have a positive attitude or teaching them to be confident when they were in a situation that was intimidating. Maybe Rachel could do this. Maybe she could be okay. Maybe she could be impressive and attractive to a man like Abe.

Abe stood very close to her. Her heart was hammering from his nearness. A slight breeze brought a blessed whiff of his soft cologne to her. She didn't know him very well, but she'd instinctively trusted him. Would he kiss her? He slowly leaned closer and she held her breath with anticipation.

He released his grip on her hand and gently wrapped his left hand around her hip. Fire seemed to burn through her from his touch. She liked how big his palm was, how big he was, nicely built and perfectly proportioned and very, very attractive. Her anticipation ramped up again, and she had to catch a long, panting breath.

Abe smiled softly and his dark eyes sparkled at her. He lifted his right hand and she felt an uncomfortable twinge for the first time around him. He wouldn't touch her scars, would he?

Tentatively he swept the hair away from her neck. Rachel jumped and pulled back away from him. For all her hopes that she was confident and ready to have a romantic interaction, she wasn't ready for him to touch her bumpy skin. Why had he gone there?

"Rachel ... I ..." He stepped in close again but the moment was shattered and her reaction was as telling as anything.

"It's fine." She stepped back again and thankfully he was enough of a gentleman to take the hint. His dark eyes looked conflicted and full of concern. She didn't like it. She wasn't some charity case, no matter how hard she was struggling. "It's fine," she repeated. "Thank you for the walk. Goodnight."

With that she turned and all but ran to her bungalow. He called to her, twice, and she could hear his footsteps approaching. She ignored him, pretending she didn't hear or feel him approaching. Finally, she reached her bungalow and tried to punch in the code. Her fingers were trembling so hard she hit the numbers wrong, twice.

"Rachel." Abe slowly approached, his voice soft as if she were a scared little filly. Rachel hated that.

She whipped around to face him but held up a hand to ward him off. "Abe it's fine. I flew through the night last night and got here early this morning." She left out the fact she'd flown on Luke's private jet and slept the entire flight. "I'm tired and want to rest. Thank you for a nice walk on the beach."

With that she turned her back on him and finally got the code typed in correctly. Shoving the door open she heard him whisper her name one more time and she thought she heard, "I'm sorry."

She slammed the door closed on his pleading voice and apology. It was fine. She was fine. The tears streaking down her face and the ache to run back outside and kiss him long and hard didn't mean anything. She swiped her face angrily and stomped to the bathroom to wash off her makeup and brush her teeth. It all meant nothing but that she needed some sleep.

CHAPTER FOUR

Abe didn't sleep well and woke early to the twittering of birds and softly rolling waves outside his open windows. His first thought was of Rachel just as it had been when he fell asleep. He groaned, rolled over, and punched the pillow. He'd messed up royally. Why had he been so stupid and attempted to brush her hair away from her scars? He'd pretended to himself that she already knew and trusted him. He'd moved too fast and damaged whatever trust she might have had for him. He knew from vicious experience how hard trust was to build, but he'd instinctively trusted Rachel.

He should've given her a tender, pure kiss, walked her back to her door, and made plans to spend today with her. Instead, he'd screwed it all up by moving too fast. He'd wanted to reveal her scars and tell her how beautiful she was to him, all of her. Obviously, he was thinking like a guy, not a girl whose perfect face had been hurt.

He honestly wondered what his motives were. He'd been

attracted by her beautiful face and shape, and for him the fact that she had scars made her that much more intriguing and appealing. Spending the short amount of time he had with her had taken that attraction to the next level. She was fun, refreshing, smart, and had a sweet humility about her he'd never seen in a woman as beautiful and accomplished as she was. He hadn't had much desire to date since Angel betrayed him and here he finally found a woman worth pursuing and he messed it up by moving too fast. Dang his natural instincts to always go hard and strong for what he wanted.

He pushed himself out of bed, dressed quickly, brushed his teeth, and grabbed a water bottle. It was five a.m. Hopefully the gym wouldn't be crowded because he really needed to pound through some weights. He drank the water as he walked along the tree-lined path to the main building. The larger bungalows, like the one he was in, were the farthest from the main area but still not too far, maybe an eighth of a mile. Preston had told him some of the guests requested shuttle service back and forth. He smiled, imagining how pampered some of those guests might be. The people he'd brought here, team leaders who'd earned the trip, were ecstatic and grateful and had literally gushed at dinner last night about how amazing the accommodations and the entire island were. His group was either getting spa treatments this morning or sleeping in and he was supposed to meet them at ten for a scuba dive. After lunch they were all doing the adventure course, ziplines, and a hike together. He'd hoped to bring Rachel. Fat lot of chance of her spending the day with him now. Would she avoid him? Should he try again to connect with her or give her some time? How much time? He was only here for a week.

He walked through the open-air main area, admiring the

smooth hardwood flooring, colorful flowerpots, and numerous water features. He found the gym connected to the spa and pushed through the glass door into an air-conditioned lobby. A young lady greeted him and offered him a towel and a water bottle. He thanked her and went through the doors to the left to the spacious, and nicely supplied gym. The wall space that wasn't windows looking out at the beautiful bay or lush jungle was mirrors. On his left were numerous cardio machines, straight in front of him various weight machines, cable machines, and racks of hand weights, on his right there was a separate room with an arched doorway and more mirrors and windows. He could see spin bikes, yoga mats, exercise balls, hand weights, and the most beautiful woman he'd ever encountered.

"Rachel," he breathed.

She had earbuds in so she must not have heard him enter. She was probably so upset about last night or so uncomfortable with him now that she was ignoring him. Her dark hair was in a long braid over her left shoulder. She squatted down low then leapt onto a box and back off. Her hair shifted and in the mirror he saw the scars on the bottom of her left cheek and her chin. She jumped back off the box and he admired the lean muscles in her legs, revealed in the mid-thigh shorts she wore.

He wanted to just stand there and watch her, admire how fit and athletic she was, but he wasn't that guy. He stepped into the arched entryway to the room and leaned against the door, hoping that was nonthreatening, but would let her know he wanted to talk if she was willing.

She was mid-jump as he moved. She stumbled, knocking her shin against the box and falling to the floor on her knees.

"Rachel!"

Abe forgot all his ideas about being relaxed and not pressuring her to talk to him as he rushed across the room and lifted her off the floor and into his arms. For one beautiful moment she sighed and leaned against him, making him feel like he was a superhero who was worthy to comfort and protect this amazing woman, but then she stiffened, pulled back, and yanked her earbuds out, tugging her braid in front of her face and neck.

He wanted to beg her to let him hold her, but he exercised the self-control that had been strengthened by his resolve to work hard. His self-control enabled him to play college sports while maintaining a four-point-oh, which was harder than he'd ever dreamt it could be. That self-control had been strengthened to nearly unbreakable in his short prison stint.

He looked her over, noting the red mark on her shin but luckily no blood. "Sorry to surprise you. Are you okay?"

She nodded stiffly, giving him a forced smile. "A little shocked to see a hulking body in the doorway."

"Hulking?" He smiled and flexed one arm, happy when his bicep popped nicely. "Like I'm the Hulk?" He lowered his voice. Maybe he could be her superhero.

She laughed and it filled up empty spaces inside of him that he hadn't fully admitted he had. He laughed with her for a few blissful seconds. When they sobered, they stood there smiling at each other.

She shifted back slightly from him, pressing her leg against the box. He took it as a bad sign but was far from admitting defeat. He'd worked hard for what he wanted; some might say pushed. The only time it had backfired was when he'd foolishly imagined he'd secured Angel's love and then she'd betrayed him and he'd ended up in prison. Eighteen months to three years in the Federal Correctional Facility in Cumberland, Maryland was looked upon as an easy stint as far as crime convictions went.

He'd been released after only three months when Angel had disappeared with millions more than it was claimed Abe ever stole and their ex-boss had finally pointed the finger in the right direction and dropped charges against Abe.

Three months. In a minimum security, white-collar crime prison. Abe knew most prisoners had it much worse but those long weeks had been purgatory. The look on his mom, dad, and sister's faces when he was arrested and each time they visited ripped the wound of misery and humiliation back open. His pastor's visits and nonstop remonstrances to "repent" for something Abe had never done. The lack of something productive to do, of a goal to achieve, of a way to improve himself. He had read hundreds of self-help and business books and been ready to start his own business the day he walked out of Hades, cursing Angel's traitorous name and planning to never trust a boss or anyone but his family again.

He shook it off and asked, "You always work out this early?"

She shrugged. "I wanted the place to myself."

"Sorry." But he wasn't sorry, not at all. He'd messed up last night. Was this his chance at redemption? Somehow he knew he could trust Rachel. She had loyalty written in her bright blue eyes. He loved that he could see the scarring on her cheek with her hair braided the way it was. He loved the way she looked in the fitted t-shirt and shorts. She was so beautiful to him. He'd heard it said, "Chicks dig scars". He didn't know about that, but he thought he dug scars, at least on her. They gave her otherwise perfect face more character and strength than even her alluring full lips and blue eyes could do.

She backed up again. "I'd better get back to my workout."

Dang. "Okay." He pointed back to the weight room. "I'll just be in there; in case you want to say hi."

She smiled as if he were cute. It wasn't all he'd hoped but better than her shutting the door on him last night, claiming she was tired and "fine".

"I'll remember that," she said.

He smiled, wanting to say so much more. Wanting to put his arms around her again and feel like he could conquer the world. Wanting to make her laugh again and see if it was the magic elixir he'd experienced earlier. Was it possible he'd found a woman who could help him heal and move past the pain and anger over Angel's betrayal? It scared him, but what was scarier was she didn't seem to feel the same. Was she shutting herself off from him because of her obvious discomfort with her burn scars, or was she simply not interested in him?

She put her earbuds back in and he took that as his sign to go. He walked to the weight room and started warming up with the cable machine, mostly because it had the best view of the aerobics room. He caught glimpses of her doing box jumps, burpees, walking lunges, and squats as he went through different back, shoulder, biceps, and triceps exercises on the cable machine and with free weights. What could he do to get her to come in here and talk to him again? Luckily, nobody else had shown up to use the facility but it was still shy of six a.m.

He smiled to himself, thinking of the mocking he'd receive from his sister, as he peeled off his t-shirt and dropped it on the weight bench next to him. He felt a little immature, which made him laugh as he was thirty-two, an ultra-successful businessman, and couldn't think of the last time he'd acted like an adolescent punk, but this move had worked for him and Preston in college. He justified that he had to at least try to get a reaction out of Rachel and he thought this might do it. Plus, maybe she'd be impressed by how hard he'd worked on his physique. A guy could hope.

He turned his back to the arched opening between the rooms, piled plenty of weight on the cable machine, and executed a reverse fly. He knew the muscles in his back were popping and hoped she'd notice. He'd sensed a fire in her, maybe his silly move would tick her off, but at this point he simply wanted a reaction from her.

His back muscles were fatiguing as he fluidly pulled through rep after rep. Maybe she wouldn't even notice. He should put his shirt back on and stop making a fool of himself. His sister would be on the floor laughing if she saw his juvenile move and knew how desperate he was to get any attention from this woman. He released the cables and his shoulders rounded. Time to admit defeat. She hadn't noticed him, or if she had, it hadn't made her want to approach him. With his track record so far with Rachel his stupid idea had probably backfired and she was less impressed than ever by him.

―――――

Rachel was almost finished with her plyometrics rounds and had convinced herself to stride into that weight room and lift some weights close to Abe. Maybe she'd pull her earbuds out and flirt with him a little. Maybe she'd see if he wanted to get breakfast together after their workout. She was dripping sweat from her last round of burpees and she noticed that the scars on her cheek were revealed and her flushed face made the white skin of the scars stand out more. Abe hadn't seemed bothered by that at all and she'd really enjoyed their comfortable banter. She'd more than enjoyed being held close to his strong chest after she fell. There was something about him, something special.

She leapt out of her last burpee and immediately dropped into jump lunges. Glancing out the opening as she jumped and switched legs, she saw a bare, broad, muscular, tanned, beautiful back in the process of executing a perfect reverse fly. She barely caught herself from tripping and crashing to the floor like she had when she'd seen Abe in the doorway earlier. Maybe she should fall. Having him hold her close had been amazing, having him do it without a shirt on would be insane.

She stopped moving completely, stared in awe for a few seconds, and then she got mad. What was he playing at? He'd had a nicely fitted t-shirt on earlier. He'd looked fabulous. Why had he stripped? To impress her? To get a reaction out of her? A sickening thought rolled through her. What if another woman was in the weight room and he was trying to impress someone else?

She stormed across the hardwood floor and through the arched entry as he released the cables. Her eyes darted around, no one but them. A smug smile crossed her face as she realized he'd taken his shirt off for her. It was adorable that this impressively successful man was trying to get her attention.

She stormed up to him, pulling out her earbuds and shoving them in a pocket of her shorts. Abe spun around and every sane thought she'd had disappeared in a poof of desire. If she'd thought his back muscles looked good, it was nothing compared to the beauty of his chest, shoulders, and abdomen, combined with his handsome face and those dark eyes looking like ... he needed her approval? How could he be humble and still look like Thor? It was the perfect combination for her.

So many things to say but she ended up sputtering. "Wh- what are you doing?"

He gave her a slow, appealing smile and folded his arms across that lovely chest. Whew! It was steamy hot in here. "Lifting. You?"

She rolled her eyes. "I was trying to have a nice little workout when I saw you all ... hot and shirtless."

His grin grew.

"And now I need to know the meaning of this. Why is your shirt off?"

He chuckled but looked a little embarrassed. Sweeping his shirt off the bench, he tugged it back on. She wanted to protest but she had already called him hot, that was more than enough. "Well, I was hoping to impress you."

"Mission accomplished," she muttered. Whirling, she stomped to the hand weights, picked up the fifteen-pound dumbbells and started a set of lateral raises.

Abe walked slowly to her. Even with his shirt on, his musculature was evident, and he was irresistible to her. He lifted a set of fifty-pound dumbbells off the rack and started slowly curling them. His bicep muscles popped so beautifully she could hardly concentrate.

"You remember in grade school when little boys used to pull your braid to get your attention?" he asked.

Rachel smiled. "Is *that* what you were doing?"

"Yes," he admitted. He kept curling but met her gaze in the mirror. "Forgive me for being immature. You do things to me."

Things? What did that mean?

"Please spend the day with me," he said in a low voice.

Rachel traded her weights for a set of twenty-pounders and did a few reps of upright rows, her stomach full of heat and anticipation at the thought of spending the day with him. The way he'd asked had been so appetizing she had no clue how to turn him down.

"Rachel?" he questioned, shelving his weights and turning to focus completely on her. "Please."

She smiled at him in the mirror. "Maybe."

"Maybe?"

"I have a few conditions."

"Such as?" A relieved smile covered his face and his dark eyes sparkled.

"Just the two of us." She hated to be selfish and monopolize his time, but she wasn't ready for a crowd.

"Of course. Anything else?"

She finished her set and put the weights down. Turning, she headed for the cable machine but said over her shoulder. "As often as possible I'd like to see that shirt off again."

Abe's deep chuckle came from behind her. "I'll see what I can do."

She winked and then tried to focus on her workout. With him working out nearby, and looking so good, it was rough.

CHAPTER FIVE

Abe was stoked that his plan had actually worked and he'd broken the ice with Rachel again. He felt a little guilty ditching his crew today, but he couldn't complain about a beautiful woman wanting to be alone with him. Yet, was it that she wanted to be alone with him or was she hiding her scars from his employees? Either way he'd take the time and hope he could grow closer to her.

He contacted each of his employees and explained that he wouldn't be with them today. They all expressed regrets but were great about it. Of course they were. Not only was he the boss and they respected him, but he also hired charismatic and hardworking team leaders who could roll with changes without making waves and didn't need him holding their hand.

He ate the acai bowl that his personal butler had delivered for him while he showered. Personal butler was an interesting concept. His was a lady from the Philippines - Alitaia, as she'd introduced herself, who was as nonintrusive as any person he'd ever met. Preston explained that if he simply texted whatever he would need throughout the day she'd make sure it happened while not intruding on his privacy. It was nice to have the service while on an all-inclusive vacation like this, but he wouldn't want to be pampered like that all the time. He was too independent. He had his house cleaned once a week back home and had food delivered when he had a particularly long day at work but for the most part, he took care of himself.

Sliding into amphibian swim trunks, a t-shirt, and socks and shoes, his thoughts quickly turned back to Rachel and he smiled thinking of her reaction to him shirtless in the gym and her asking to see him that way more. She was confident and sassy under the pain of her injuries. He wanted to help her see how beautiful she was through his eyes. He'd been independent and alone for so long it was surprising how much he craved her company. It was like when he discovered the Rolling Stones as a teenager and realized he'd never tire of their music, as opposed to all the punk bands he used to listen to. He never had. Would he ever tire of time with Rachel? He doubted it.

He and Rachel planned to meet outside her bungalow at eight. He was a few minutes early, but she was waiting outside wearing a short-sleeved, high-necked rash guard with shorts covering her swim bottoms. Her long braid was in front of her neck, but he could see a little of the scarring on her cheek and chin. He'd seen women in skimpy bikinis who didn't look as appealing as she did in her modest suit.

"Hey," he said, walking up to her.

"Hey." She raised a hand.

"What do you want to try first?"

"I want to do it all!" She grinned, her blue eyes sparkling with excitement.

Abe chuckled and took her hand. "All right. It's going to be a busy day."

She laughed.

"How about the adventure course first?" He had some ulterior motives. His group was doing scuba and beach activities this morning then adventure course and ziplines in the afternoon. If he could flip flop that with Rachel, he wouldn't run into them and would give her the privacy she seemed to desire. He'd proudly show her off as his date to any of them but was concerned about how she might react to the group, who would be intrigued by her and want his attention as well.

"Perfect."

They walked hand in hand along the trails, following the signs that led to the adventure course. They talked easily about her family and a little about his. He could talk with her all day. He wondered at what point he should share that he'd been framed for embezzling by his ex-fiancée and spent time in prison. She might already know the story if she'd dug through a Google search on him.

The adventure course was fun and at times challenging. Abe especially liked watching Rachel navigate it, see the muscles in her lean legs and arms flex. He also thought it was cute to watch the helpers on the course tease and flirt with her. She laughed and chatted easily with them, her beautiful blue eyes glinting with good humor. Abe wasn't a jealous-type person and he knew he didn't need to be with Rachel. She was simply being friendly with the young men who were helping them, and she also reassured Abe that she was interested in him as she kept catching his eye and gifting him with beautiful smiles. How could he possibly blame the guys for flirting with her? She was incredible.

At the end of the adventure course they took the option to

walk up the steep stairs to a platform that started the first zipline through the trees. There was a series of ziplines, some above the tree line, some through the trees. Abe enjoyed flying over the tropical jungle like Tarzan, if only he could be holding Rachel while he did it. He smiled and focused on the ride. At the end of the zipline course there was a forty-foot freefall onto a massive cushion.

Rachel waited for him at the top of final platform. Her smile was a fraction what it had been all morning.

"You okay?" he asked, instinctively reaching for her hand.

She squeezed his hand tight. "I don't mind heights and ziplines, but I'm not a huge fan of free falls."

"You don't have to do it," he said quickly, wanting to reassure her she had nothing to prove to him.

Glancing at him, she pulled the side of her lower lip between her teeth and he lost all ability to think rationally. The two young men who'd been with them throughout the adventure course and the ziplines were waiting and watching but Abe was going to pull her close and taste that bottom lip himself.

As he reached for her she gripped his hand tighter and said, "Together?"

Oh, right. They were at the top of a free fall and not in the spot to be sharing their first kiss. It had been too long since Abe had been serious about any woman and he was falling hard and fast for this one. Focusing on his trust issues or any kind of rational thought wasn't really any competition for all the Rachel fantasies floating through his brain.

Abe nodded, hoping there would be time later to fulfill his dreams of kissing her. "Together," he agreed.

They held hands and one of the young guys behind them said, "I'll count for you. 3 ... 2 ... 1!"

Rachel gave him the most appealing smile and then she launched herself forward. Abe leapt to keep up, but their hands were ripped apart. She screamed out a half-giggle, half cry of shock as she fell, and he couldn't help but chuckle at how cute she was as he fell. They landed on the cushion, bounced a couple of times, and then settled. Rachel rolled toward him and right into his arms. Perfect.

Abe grinned at her. "Great job."

"Yes, it was, wasn't it?"

Her hair was purposely braided to semi-cover her face, but it had been pushed aside. He resisted the urge to push it out of the way and kiss her scars and then kiss her lips and then tell her how incredible she was to him.

"That was fun." She laughed and scrambled out of his arms before sliding off the mat and onto the ground. Fun? Abe would show her fun. Instead of acting on the overwhelming desire to grab her and kiss her, Abe followed her off the mat. Their guides jumped down to meet them shortly after.

Abe shook each of their hands, feeling awkward that he didn't have cash to tip them but Preston had been insistent that he not carry money and just enjoy all the experiences, worry about tips at the end if he wanted. It was kind of freeing, but Abe liked tipping, partly because it showed gratitude for a job well done and partly because it showed how generous he could be. He'd come from a solid family but there hadn't been extra money. Now that he had it, Abe liked to share his wealth. He knew it was also a prideful streak in him, it felt good to have extra money to bequeath on others.

"Where to next?" he asked Rachel, instinctively taking her hand.

She looked down at their joined hands then up at him.

"Carlos said the waterfall hike is only a mile. Do you want to do that?"

"Sure."

They grabbed water bottles from their guides and set off on the trail to the waterfall. It was a beautiful trek with thick trees and bushes lining the trail. Within minutes a babbling creek trickled beside them.

"So, you grew up in Jackson Hole, Wyoming?" he asked. She'd told him about each of her siblings but only briefly mentioned where they'd lived.

"For the most part, but we spent time in Vermont, Puerto Rico, and Georgia. My mom liked to follow the sun. As soon as Eve started college she started the schedule of Vermont in the fall, Puerto Rico in the winter, Savannah Georgia in the spring and Jackson Hole in the summer."

"Sounds like a great plan." His parents could barely afford one middle-class home in Rochester. They didn't like that he'd paid their home off, hired contractors to do every upgrade and expansion his mom had ever dreamt about, and put millions into their account so they could retire and travel. Neither of them complained about being able to support his sister in her acting career.

"I think they've enjoyed it, until ..." Her mouth pursed and she focused on the stream. "They started rebuilding the Jackson house, but it won't be done for this summer and because of me they spent most of the winter in Vermont."

Their footsteps and the stream were the only sounds for a few seconds as he debated if he dared go deeper into the explosion and her pain. "I'm so sorry about the explosion," he murmured, gazing at her profile. He noticed she kept him on her right side whenever possible.

"Me too," she grunted out.

"Do you feel like you're ... recovering all right?"

She glanced at him. "Yep. Doing awesome, great, perfect." Her smile was the fakest he'd seen on her. How he thought he knew her so well after one day should've been a question to dwell on. Instead, he tugged her to a stop on the trail, put both hands on her waist, and turned her to him.

"Would you lie to me?" he asked.

Her eyebrows arched. "No. I'm not a liar."

"Would you lie about how you're doing?" He was pushing it, but he found he couldn't help himself. He wanted to be there for her, help her, and he felt like he knew exactly what she needed.

"All day long," she said, jutting out her chin.

She was so brave and amazing, yet there was a glint in her blue eyes, a glint of pain and humiliation and anger at the injustice of some idiot blowing up her parents' home to get back at her brother, and Rachel being caught in the crossfire. Abe felt like he could empathize. He'd felt similar when he'd been wrongly accused and thrown in prison. He'd been certain his future had been ripped apart, but he'd gotten through it and was stronger because of his experiences. He might never forgive Angel but that was another story.

Abe wanted to help Rachel get past her pain. He questioned his judgment, but only for a second. He knew he was being braver than facing down thugs in prison as he gently pulled her into his arms. Rachel let out a small noise of surprise and was stiff and unyielding for long enough he almost released her and groveled until she forgave him for his impetuous move and hopefully didn't back out of her agreement to spend the day with him.

The moment when she relaxed against him, wrapped her

arms around his lower back, and laid her head against his chest was a better victory than the national championship his junior year of college. They stood quietly on that trail, holding on to each other for a long time. Abe wanted to murmur comforting words and platitudes, but he imagined she'd heard them all. He remembered when he was in prison and some buddies, including Preston, came by to visit. They meant well but all the well-meaning condolences and empty "it wasn't your faults" really just ticked him off. He felt guilty being mad at his friends, even at the time, but the pain and anger just wasn't something you could talk through and make better. His hatred of Angel wasn't something he let himself dwell on, but it still had festered throughout the years. Maybe since all he'd tried to do was bury it and not deal with it.

Abe could've held her all day but Rachel shifted, glanced up at him, and murmured, "Thank you. I think that was more effective than months of therapy."

Abe gave her a soft smile. "Anytime."

She smiled at him and he knew she meant her words and believed his. Holding Rachel was definitely not a hardship for him. He was quickly becoming attached to her. Would she let him into her life, into her heart? Was he ready for that after he thought he'd suffered the ultimate betrayal? It had been ten years but he'd let the anger and resentment chafe and grow like an infected splinter that he refused to remove. Sometimes he wondered how he'd to let it all go so he could have a healthy relationship. Could he let it go? For Rachel? He wanted to think he'd do anything for her but forgiving Angel and moving on had always been a taller order than he'd been capable of.

Rachel loved every minute of the day spent with Abe. They'd swum in the small waterfall pool then had lunch on a private table near the outdoor pools. After lunch they'd done a scuba dive in the quiet bay. Rachel thought she'd be humiliated adjusting the mask over her face but it was above her scars and her rash guard covered her shoulders and part of her neck and her long braid covered the worst of the scarring on her neck and chin. Though some of the employees' eyes throughout the day had flitted to the scars on her cheek, that she could only hide with her hair long and flowing, they didn't stay there and they were all friendly and fun with her. More importantly Abe never so much as flinched when he glimpsed the scars. He acted like he almost thought they were ... attractive? At the very least, they definitely didn't seem to bother him. At best, he seemed to like the variety in her face. How amazing would that be?

They'd barely begun their dive when she noticed Abe was descending much too quickly. Rachel was an experienced diver, and one glance at his eyes through his mask told her the pressure was building in his head. She'd grabbed him by the arm and quickly removed a weight from his belt and dropped it to the ocean floor then waited while he equalized. After the dive, the scuba instructor and Abe had praised her quick action and Abe kept saying she was his hero, which made her smile. She could admit to herself she liked her ability to react quick and she liked being with Abe.

After they removed their scuba equipment and handed it over to the instructor they swam in the ocean for a while then relaxed in cushioned chaise lounges beside the private infinity pool outside of Abe's bungalow overlooking the beach. If this two-story fabulous suite of rooms could be called a bungalow. She enjoyed the tropical air and the beautiful view. Mostly, her view of Abe. She took a sip of a strawberry daquiri and stared at him.

He lifted his sunglasses and winked at her. "Liking the view?"

"Very much." His shirt was off, and she thought he was glorious.

He chuckled and leaned up on one elbow. "So, you wanted to do 'everything' today. What are we missing? What should we do next?"

She tilted her head, liking that he was adventurous. Her brothers would like him. Her brothers would also like that when Abe was around she rarely thought about her scarring. When he'd held her in his arms on the trail leading to the waterfall she'd felt a sort of healing power from his touch. She'd thought it was a little piece of heaven. Could she heal emotionally and spiritually enough to feel worthy to be with someone like Abe? It was cliché but sometimes she blamed her Heavenly Father for not protecting her from the bomb. She hated when she had those dark thoughts, but they were still there.

"Maybe we could just relax the rest of the afternoon, have dinner together, and then go on another walk on the beach." Her stomach pitched happily at the thought. She would kiss him tonight. What if he tried to push her hair away again? Maybe she'd let him. If her scars didn't repulse him, why should she be freaking out about them? Still, her stomach tightened at the thought of him looking at them, touching them.

"So, when are we going to bike around all the island trails, go deep-sea fishing, and try out all the services the spa offers?"

She smiled and lifted her right shoulder. "There's always tomorrow."

His slow grin made her stomach fill up with happy bubbles. "So you're saying I get to spend another day with you?"

"I think I may grant you that privilege."

"Thank you." His warm look seemed to sear through her. "What if I lobby for other 'privileges'?"

She laughed but it sounded shaky. What privileges? Kissing? She was definitely on board for some kissing. "We'll see."

He winked and then put his sunglasses back on and reclined into the chair.

The rest of the day flew by too quickly for Rachel. She loved this alternate reality she was living in and she loved not worrying about a future that had been changed by the bombing. Had she let her scars define her? She would've thought she'd be stronger than that but getting back out and facing the world with a deformed face had proven tougher than she'd imagined it would be. Nobody wanted to be the lawyer trying to help children, but who was also giving them nightmares. On the other hand, maybe those women were wrong. She'd trusted in their words because of their status with the law school, how impressed she'd been with them when she met them, and the fact that they didn't know she was there and weren't being catty, simply discussing their concerns. Now she was wondering if maybe her scars weren't as bad as she'd feared. It was obvious to Abe they weren't. Abe made her feel more beautiful than any man had, and it didn't seem like her scars bothered him at all.

She and Abe separated to shower and get ready, then had dinner delivered to his bungalow. She wore a simple wrap dress that covered her left shoulder and her hair was swept to the left to cover her chin and neck. Some of the scars on her cheek showed as she hadn't draped her hair so severely to the left. Would Abe notice that she was growing more confident around him? What if she saw in his eyes that her scars looked disgusting? She pushed that worry away, focusing on confidence and how great Abe had been so far.

She bravely rapped on his bungalow door and it swung open quickly as if he'd been waiting for her. He looked incredibly appealing in a short-sleeved white button-down shirt and tan pants that set off his dark coloring. His deep-brown eyes were fascinating to her.

"Rachel," he said softly. His eyes swept over her carefully, slowly, as if he had to slow down his gaze and appreciate each inch of her. Rachel found herself flushing with pleasure from his look. She'd kept herself hidden from everyone but her family and a few close friends the past eight months, since the bombing, except for the failure at Harvard Law. Had she been silly to stew and worry so much? Would most people not care or was Abe simply special? She was pretty certain Abe was incredibly special.

He took her hand in his and led her inside. She felt as if she were a princess given the tender way he treated her.

Dinner was all laid out, a seafood feast of shrimp, lobster, and crab. They sat and Abe offered a prayer before eating. She didn't ask him about his faith but liked that it was part of him. As they ate, they talked about the incredible island, the highlights from today, and what they wanted to do tomorrow.

As they finished eating, she said, "I'm sorry I've kept you from your group today."

He shook his head quickly and took a drink of his water. "Don't be. They're fine. They earned this incredible trip, not the right to have me by their side every minute."

She tilted her head to the left and felt her hair sweep down her arm. "But who wouldn't want you by their side every minute?"

He arched his eyebrows and gave her a confident smirk. "Good point. I'm sure everyone would." He laughed to show he was teasing.

She smiled. "I know I would."

Abe's gaze sharpened on her. "Are you finished?" he asked quietly.

She nodded, swallowing at the intensity in his dark eyes. Abe was the type of man who worked hard for what he wanted and didn't give up until he had it. Was *she* what he wanted? The very idea sent a thrill through her.

Abe stood and extended his hand. She took it and let him pull her to her feet. In silent agreement they walked out of his incredible bungalow through the open patio, past the glowing infinity pool, and down to the beach. They stopped in the soft sand. A wave rolled onto the sand, the light from the moon and his bungalow lent a romantic glow. Rachel couldn't keep her eyes off Abe's handsome face.

He wrapped his hands around her hips and stared down at her. "You're so incredibly beautiful, Rachel." His voice was low and husky and she felt every syllable sink deep into her heart. She'd heard similar words from many men, before the accident. Hearing them from Abe now meant the world to her.

"Thank you," she said. Part of her wanted to push her hair from her face and neck and ask him directly: did he really think she was beautiful with the scars. Most of her wanted to forget the issues she faced and simply experience what she knew would be an incredible kiss with this even more incredible man. So instead of worrying or questioning she slid her arms around his neck and smiled encouragingly at him.

Abe's gaze deepened and she could easily read the question in his eyes, did she want his kiss, did she want him? No matter how successful, intense, or driven he was, she knew he'd never take anything from her she wasn't ready to give. She nodded and breathed out, "Yes, please," even though he'd never asked a verbal question.

Abe let out a breath that seemed to shake his large frame. Then he wasted no more time. His hands slid around to cup her lower back with his large palms, he pulled her tight against him, and he bent and claimed her lips with his own.

Rachel's mouth and body responded just as quickly. She threaded her fingers through his hair and returned his kiss with more desire and joy than she'd ever felt in a man's arms. The kiss became a communication of needs, wants, hopes, and dreams. She shared more with him in that kiss than she'd ever wanted to share with a man before.

When Abe pulled back and rested his forehead against hers, they were both panting for air.

"Rach," he said in a soft whisper. He raised both hands as if to cup her face but then his eyes widened slightly and he dropped his hands back to her waist.

Rachel wished she could tell him it was okay, he could touch her face, he could move her hair away, he could look at her scars. She trusted him to do it all, but instead of getting into that, she simply enjoyed the moment, pulled his head down to hers, and kissed him all over again. They could deal with her issues later. Thank heavens he didn't have any issues.

CHAPTER SIX

A be was happy to spend another adventure-filled day with Rachel but could hardly wait for the nighttime to come. Last night they'd kissed for a long time and he'd finally forced himself to walk her back to her bungalow so he didn't push her too fast. She was strong and brave, he knew that, but she'd also been through something horrific and was still recovering. He didn't want to damage her fledgling trust in him and kissing her was so intense and all-encompassing he actually feared his iron self-control might slip when he had her in his arms.

He really wanted to kiss her again but he also wanted to hold her close and talk through her healing, her scars, and see if he could help her accept them. He wanted to tell her about his past, his resentment, and have her help him heal as well. He wanted more than this week of vacation with her. He wanted to develop a relationship, make Rachel Jewel a part of his life, a big part. He was concerned though. Would his trust issues and bottled resentment at Angel rear its ugly head? *Wounds buried alive never die*, was his a saying his mom repeated and it was true. His anger at Angel was buried but sadly still there. More importantly, was Rachel ready to commit to him? He might be a rebound relationship for her, not from another man but from her accident. He didn't want that. He wanted her.

They started their day with a run around the entire perimeter of the island. A couple of times they hit rocky outcroppings on the beach and had to work their way over or around them, which added to the fun and didn't slow Rachel down at all. He loved how adventurous, fit, and fun she was. Had she shut that part of herself down since the accident as well? She seemed like a little child at Christmas as they did different adventures.

After breakfast they went out on a deep-sea fishing excursion with a couple twenty-year old guides from Belize who were hilarious and couldn't stop looking at Rachel. Abe didn't feel any jealousy but he did have this odd urge to cover up her long, shapely legs, kind of similar to how he felt when men checked out his little sister, yet with Rachel he wanted to be the one checking her out.

The experience was pretty lame as far as fishing trips went. They only got a few bites in four hours, but simply being around the bewitching, adorable, beautiful Rachel and then watching her face glow with excitement when she fought with, and reeled in, a twenty-pound tuna made it the most exciting fishing trip he'd ever been on.

One thing he'd noticed yesterday, and she did again with their fishing buddies, was she really focused on them. Asked about their families, past experiences, education, hobbies, how they ended up here, what they thought about the island and their work, etc. She was incredibly thoughtful and friendly, which was impressive to him as he'd initially sensed she didn't want to be around unknown people staring at her scars, but for some reason he sensed an underlying need to know if her brother Luke's employees were happy and well taken care of. Was Preston right and she was spying on him? Abe shook the thought away. It didn't seem like Rachel would do that and what reason would she have to? Preston was an amazing employee and manager.

After a late lunch at his bungalow they went on a bike ride, exploring all the trails through the jungle and going back to the waterfall again, where they ran into his group. It was bound to happen, but he had been dead-on about how great his employees were. They all greeted Rachel with warm enthusiasm, chatted for a while with them, and then let him and Rachel go on their way. Maybe tomorrow he'd spend more time with them. He glanced over at Rachel as they pedaled sedately along a wide part of the trail and she grinned at him. Then again, maybe not. No one could blame him for craving every minute he could get alone with her.

He was getting ready for dinner when a rap came at his door. Buttoning his shirt and thinking maybe Rachel was early, he hurried to the door. He swung it wide and grinned. "Hey ... oh hey."

Preston smiled and arched an eyebrow. "Not who you were expecting? I hear you've spent every spare minute with Rachel Jewel."

Abe nodded. "It's been fabulous." He gestured for his friend to come in.

"Sorry, no time, I've got a dinner appointment with my own beautiful lady."

"Anybody I know?"

Preston's blue eyes flashed but his smile was smooth. "Nope. Just a beautiful single guest. I just wanted to let you know that there's a storm warning for tonight. It should pass by morning, but you might want to cuddle with the beautiful Miss Jewel and keep her safe." He winked. "There are candles and flashlights in this closet." He pointed to a closet next to the door.

"Thanks for coming by yourself," Abe said. As the manager Preston had plenty to keep him busy, but he'd taken the time to tell an old friend that a storm was coming.

"Of course." His eyes darkened a little bit. "Hey, not to sound ... unconfident, but has Rachel said anything about the resort or how I'm running it or what her brother is thinking? It's kind of unnerving to go through a change in ownership and I haven't had the opportunity to meet my new boss in person yet."

Ah, this was why Preston had come. Preston was a tremendously hard worker, but he wasn't the guy who was going to be self-employed. The embezzlement nightmare had affected not just Abe and Angel, but Preston as well. Preston had worked with them for McKnight and he'd lost his job, even though he'd done nothing wrong besides being close to Abe and Angel. He'd lifted himself back on his feet and had worked his way into resort management, running different resorts in the Caribbean and securing this incredible spot over four years ago. He seemed to love what he did here but Abe could understand him being uneasy about an ownership change. Abe was grateful that he was his own man and didn't have to worry about a boss, but he remembered those feelings with that first job after college that had gone so horribly wrong.

"She hasn't said anything about you or her brother in regard to the island but I know she loves it here." He didn't know how to tell Preston that she did kind of quiz each employee, but he felt like that was just Rachel being interested in people and their stories. It was nothing to concern his friend about. "She's commented plenty about how fabulous the resort is and how great the staff are." Abe clapped his friend on the shoulder. "This place is incredible and you're doing an amazing job. You shouldn't worry."

Preston smiled but still looked uneasy. "Thanks. If you hear anything ..."

"I'll let you know," Abe filled in for him. They'd been friends since before college, of course he'd let him know if there were any real red flags from Rachel about Preston and his work performance. His friend had worked hard to reach this spot and Abe was loyal to him.

"Thanks." Preston backed away. "Enjoy your night."

"I will." Abe lifted a hand. "You too."

"You know me." Preston pumped his eyebrows, turned, and walked away.

Abe shut the door and smiled to himself. Preston didn't need to worry, this island was the most amazing vacation Abe had ever been on and as he thought about it, all the employees had responded very positively about their work here. Plus, Abe would definitely, definitely enjoy this night. He'd be with Rachel. What could possibly be more enjoyable?

Rachel walked along the tiki-lit path toward Abe's bungalow. Excitement pulsed through her at the thought of being with him, but she felt a little apprehension as well. She was wearing a fitted, pale blue dress. For this trip she'd only brought her new tailored formals that covered her left shoulder, leaving her right shoulder bare. The style covered as much of her scarring as possible and focused the eye to the smooth skin of her right side. Crazily enough, she wished she'd brought one of her older dresses that showed off both shoulders.

She tossed her long hair back and realized that showing as much of the scars as she was currently doing, was brave enough for tonight. Her hair was styled in long curls and draped down her back. For the first time since her experience at the law school and around someone other than her family, she was willingly revealing her face and neck. When she'd gotten ready tonight she'd put on lighter makeup than she usually would for a dinner date and styled her hair to reveal her scarring instead of hiding it. Her scars didn't look as repulsive to her tonight. Was she seeing herself through Abe's eyes? Would he still tell her she was incredibly beautiful or would his gaze get stuck on the scarring and not be able to drag away?

She pressed a hand to her stomach and said a prayer in her head. Abe was amazing. He'd love her, all of her. She gasped as she realized what she'd just thought. Love? They hadn't known each other long enough for love. She knew she wanted more time with Abe and that this relationship could easily grow to love and beyond.

"Rachel?" a man's voice said from a path to the side.

Her head darted that way and she saw Preston approaching. She hadn't done as thorough of a job researching him as she should have the past two days. Though she'd talked with every employee she encountered, she hadn't hacked into his personal computer and combed through his accounting, like she had planned. She smiled to herself, knowing Luke would never have her do something like that and also realizing she'd been too busy enjoying time with Abe. She knew Luke would be thrilled at her emotional progress and not care at all that she hadn't gone to the extreme with her duties, but it irked her to not have followed through the way she usually would.

"Preston," she said.

He extended his hand and she shook his briefly. His eyes went to her scars and lingered. Her stomach dropped in horror. It was the exact reaction she'd dreaded since seeing the scars herself. It reminded her of the long recovery, the horrifically painful process of peeling off the skin layers to reveal new skin underneath and hoping each time it wouldn't be as ugly, but it always seemed to be more puckered and repulsive to her.

Would Abe react the same? She didn't think so and she was sick of hiding. She tilted her chin imperiously and straightened her shoulders. Preston finally dragged his eyes from her left side, though it seemed to take enormous effort for him to refocus on her face.

He cleared his throat, shifted his feet, and murmured, "How are you enjoying your stay?"

"It's amazing. This island is the most incredible vacation I've ever been on." The second best was a camping trip with all of her siblings through Glacier National Park a year before Eve had rushed into marriage with a snake and Paisley had been born. They'd roughed it, but loved every minute being together in the beauty of nature.

"That's saying something." He smiled more fully. "I'm sure the Jewel family has been on some incredible vacations. Doesn't your brother Joshua own resorts all over the world?"

"Yeah." She nodded. "Don't tell him that Luke beat him on this one."

He chuckled, finally not gawking at her scars. "I won't, but

I'm glad to hear it. Anything I can do to make your stay more pleasant?"

"No. Thank you for asking. It's been just about perfect." She wondered what he knew about her and Abe. The two men were friends. She realized as she stared at Preston that she'd been negligent in not only scoping out his personal and work life more diligently, she'd never Googled Abe Bradford to see what skeletons might be in his past. She smiled to herself, doubting there would be any. Abe was good through and through. She didn't think she would Google him as the only thing she'd probably find was his path to success and women clinging to him. She had no desire to see him with another woman. In her mind, Abe was custom made to be all hers.

She focused back on Preston, wishing she knew how to bring up the woman she'd overheard him with the first night she'd been here. His "angel love". She'd semi-forgotten about the interaction and seeing him again piqued her curiosity, especially wondering who the pair were trying to steal money from. She'd texted the info to Luke, but he hadn't had any idea who the two might be scamming.

"I've got to run but hope to see more of you." He smiled. "I told Abe, and I'm assuming you're on your way to his bungalow ..." He let that linger in the warm air.

She nodded, no reason to hide it, but she didn't like the innuendo behind his words.

"There's a tropical storm blowing in. No reason to worry, but maybe just stay hunkered down tonight." He gave her a knowing smile as if she'd hunker down with Abe all night. She wanted to explain that she'd kiss Abe aplenty, but she'd spend the night in her own bed.

Instead, she simply waved a hand and murmured "thank you"

before walking away. As she turned onto the path to Abe's bungalow she felt eyes burning a hole through her back. Glancing around, she saw only a shadow flitting away. A chill ran through her. Was that Preston or someone else? She'd felt completely safe on this gorgeous island. If it had been Preston, why had he stayed and watched her walk away when he'd claimed to be in a hurry?

She ignored those worries and knocked on Abe's door.

Abe swung the door wide, his grin even wider. His eyes swept over her face and dress but then he did a double take at what she was revealing. His gaze slowed down and traveled carefully over every inch of her face and neck. He focused in on her eyes and the tenderness and appreciation she saw written there made her legs turn to mush. If there could be a complete opposite reaction to Preston's, this was it.

"Rachel," he breathed. He swallowed and then murmured, "Do you have any idea how beautiful you are?"

Rachel's legs got even weaker. "Thank you," she managed through a throat filled with emotion.

Abe gently wrapped his hands around her hips and tugged her into the open main area of his bungalow. He toed the door shut, fully focused on her. Rachel's heart thumped faster and she was having a hard time catching a full breath.

Abe took his time, as if he had all night to appreciate her. He slid his hands around to her back and gently stroked them up her back and across her shoulders. His touch was feather light as he ran his fingers across her neck and then cupped her cheeks with his palms, touching her scars and not seeming repulsed at all. In fact he appeared to be savoring the feel of her.

Rachel didn't want to cry right now. She wanted to simply

enjoy his touch, but emotion was welling in her throat and stinging at her eyes.

"So beautiful," he murmured, placing a soft kiss on her lips.

Rachel cleared her throat and had to know. "I appreciate you accepting the scars but you can't mean that they're ... beautiful."

"I do, Rach," he said earnestly, staring at her with determination and tenderness in his gaze. "The scars aren't the smooth, perfect skin of the rest of your face, but they give you character, strength, and they make you even more appealing and beautiful to me. You're gorgeous, perfect, tantalizing, attractive, appealing—"

Rachel kissed him then. She kissed him long and hard and she was transported to the light and beauty that she'd longed for this past eight months.

She pulled back and smiled at him and immediately Abe started saying, "Charming, sexy, striking, irresistible, enticing—"

Rachel laughed and interrupted him by kissing him again. Abe smiled against her lips but then the kisses picked up in intensity. He ran his hands down her neck, along her shoulders, and then down her sides. She shivered as delicious goosebumps erupted everywhere he touched. He wrapped those large hands around her waist and picked her up off the ground, pushing her up against the wall and kissing her passionately. Rachel was glad he was holding her because she couldn't have supported her own weight at this point. She was head over heels for him and only wanted more of this, more time with him, more of Abe.

When neither of them could catch a breath he set her on the ground and stroked his fingers over her skin.

"It smells good," she said, teasing him. The dinner was apparently ready and waiting. "Were we planning on eating sometime tonight?"

He chuckled but then grew serious. "Being with you, seeing all of you. Ah, Rach. I can't think of food, I can't think of anything but you. I just want to look at you, kiss you, hold you."

Rachel smiled, loving his sweet words. She leaned closer and challenged him, "Go for it."

He grinned and started with the kissing. She knew eventually they'd have to stop and eat and sometime tonight she'd have to go back to her own bungalow. As a strong breeze swept through the open windows and doors, she thought she'd wait until the storm got really awful. Nothing was going to pull her away from this man. Nothing.

CHAPTER SEVEN

A warm tropical rain was falling, and the wind was stirring up debris around their ankles when Abe walked Rachel back to her bungalow. She'd teased him that it was only a few hundred yards away but he insisted. She was crushing so hard on him, but she had no clue how this thrilling ride would end. They could spend the next few days together but then what? Vacation would be over and he would have to go back to work. The only good news was she hadn't committed to a job, starting her own business, or if she'd brave her dreams of law school and family law yet. Maybe she could move to Buffalo, take the time she needed to get to know him. Who knew, but she liked the possibilities.

Abe stopped at the small porch overhang of her bungalow. His gaze was intense on her. He said in a low, rough voice, "I'd better leave you here. I'm afraid if I kiss you in there I won't be able to walk away."

A thrill ran through her at his implication. She also loved

that he knew his limits and wasn't going to push them. "That's probably smart of you. If you thought Caleb was tough at lacrosse you should see how well all five of my brothers perform in a fistfight." She winked to show she was teasing. She didn't think her brothers would fight him. Well ... they did love to fight and had always been a little overprotective of her and Eve. Especially since her accident. Actually, they'd always been over the top with Eve because she was so sweet, and if any of them found out who Paisley's real father was, the guy would probably be ripped into pieces.

He nodded solemnly. "I'd let them thump me if I ever disrespected you."

"Abe." She threw her arms around his neck and kissed him. She could've kept kissing him, no matter the rain or the wind or the worries over kissing too much, but Abe pulled back, gently removed her arms from his neck and backed away.

"I'll see you in the morning," he promised.

She nodded. "I bet you can't wait."

His gaze was intense as he nodded. "I can't. Please punch in your code so I know you get inside safe."

She smiled and obeyed, pushing the door open and raising a hand in farewell. She didn't have time to sit and sigh over how incredible he was. As soon as she stepped inside, she heard her phone ringing. She'd left it here, hardly using it the past few days.

Running to grab it before she missed the call, she saw it was Luke.

"Hey, big brother."

"Rach. How are you?"

"So good. This place is insane! You and Mar have to come. I

was telling Preston how you beat Joshua on this one, it's the coolest vacation spot I've ever been to."

He chuckled. "I'm glad. Thanks, sis. Hey, how bad's the storm?"

She peered out her windows. "It's just raining and some wind. I've seen a lot worse."

"That's good. Keep an eye out for me. The weather service that watches over the island contacted me because Preston wasn't responding. They're worried it might reach a category one hurricane."

"Truly? How bad is that?" Rachel had been on a lot of tropical vacations and lived in Puerto Rico with her family for short stints, but she'd never been through a hurricane. March wasn't typically hurricane season so she hadn't even given a bad storm a thought.

"Worst case, the winds could get up to ninety-five miles per hour so you definitely wouldn't want to be out in it, but that's absolutely worst case. The buildings there are built to withstand hurricanes, and the rest of my staff are aware and are trying to find Preston. If it gets horrible there's a storm shelter below the fitness rooms."

"Gotcha."

"No worries, I'm sure it won't progress past a tropical storm. Hurricanes are rare in the spring in the Caribbean. It's just odd they can't find Preston and I wanted to make sure you were safe."

"Thanks. I'm great right now." She rushed to tell him the little news she had. "So I've quizzed every employee I've interacted with and they all seem happy and content, not a one would breathe a word against Preston. Interesting, huh? Especially after that conversation I overheard."

"That was odd and disturbing. So obviously, he and this woman have stolen from someone before and she'd go to prison if the person saw her. Hmm. Makes me think my manager would likely be stealing from me also, but that's good the employees are happy."

There was a long pause. Luke was thinking and she let him do it. When he spoke, instead of expounding on Preston and his worries of embezzlement he said, "What else have you been up to? This is going to sound cheesy, but your voice sounds as happy as Mar's when she talks about me." There was an obvious tease in his voice, but it was also full of hope. She knew how much all of her family had worried about her the past eight months. Luke would be very happy to know she was doing so well, and maybe had found her special someone like all of her brothers had been busy doing the past year.

"The truth is ... I met someone."

"Really?"

"Yeah. He's great. We've spent the past two days together. I like him a lot."

"How much is a lot?"

She cleared her throat and admitted, "I wore my hair back from my face tonight for dinner. He touched my scars and told me how beautiful I am." Maybe it was too much information, but she was an open book with her family.

"Ah, sis." Luke cleared his throat. "That's so great. We've all been praying you'd know how beautiful, smart, and impressive you are. The scars don't change that one bit."

"Thanks, Luke." Now that she was allowing herself to heal and believe she would be okay she could truthfully say she felt their prayers and could internalize their belief in her. Interesting how before when she was feeling bitter inside she hadn't felt much of anything but the pressing fears and darkness. She remembered her mom saying the Lord's hand was always outstretched and they had to choose to put their hand out to feel the blessings he was waiting to bestow. Abe was definitely a blessing she hadn't seen coming and was even more of a blessing than she could ever have hoped for. One dark thought still lingered though. Someday, somehow she had to forgive Flint Brooks and put the accident completely behind her. That was a tough thought. She'd have to request more prayers from her family.

"I can't wait to meet him," Luke said. "What's his name so I can research him to make sure he's worthy of my sister?"

Rachel laughed. "There are no worries there, he's the best."

"His name?"

Rachel smiled, not stressed at all about what Luke might find. Abe was perfect in her eyes. Her only stress was how to spend more time with him after they left the island. "Abe Bradford."

"Abe Bradford?" He paused for a second then said, "Big guy? Played lacrosse against Caleb?"

"Yeah. Why?" She'd pushed to the back of her mind Abe's distant connection to Caleb, but something in Luke's voice set her on edge. Had Abe been a jerk on the lacrosse field? Luke couldn't possibly know something bad about Abe. There couldn't be anything. Cold sweat pricked her brow. Abe simply had to be as good as she believed.

"There was something about him in the news years ago. I just remember because I'd watched him play against Caleb and been impressed. He was a great defender."

"The name probably stuck because he's a fellow billionaire. You guys all stick together, right?" She tried to tease but her stomach was tumbling. Something about him in the news? The news rarely reported anything positive.

Luke chuckled. "That's right. If he's a 'fellow billionaire' he must be a good guy." His voice was full of irony. Luke was not caught up on status or money and he didn't treat people differently based on their income. "I'm remembering something, but I definitely need to look into it and get the right details. Hold on while I Google him."

She clutched the phone uneasily, begging her Father above like she hadn't begged since she woke up from surgery after the explosion and found out her life would never be the same. *Please let Abe be the man I think he is. Please.* She'd fallen so hard for him, the thought of something being off with Abe was inconceivable. Yet there was a niggling worry in the back of her mind. She'd never taken the time to research him like she usually would. They were on this exotic island, removed from the world, and she was so far off her dating game from years past that maybe she'd been too innocent, too trusting. Abe had to be good. He just had to be. Hadn't she been through enough pain with her face and her life being torn apart? If Abe wasn't good ...

"Yeah, sis ..." Luke pushed out a breath. "You might want to pull up your computer and read all of this yourself. The internet is really good on the island because of the satellite system I pay to be part of."

Rachel didn't really care about the internet connection. "What about Abe?" Her voice came out in a high squeak. Luke had found something bad enough he'd rather have her read it herself? Why wouldn't he just share it with her?

"It's not bad," he hastened to say. "Okay, it's bad, but he was wrongly accused. I mean you hope he was wrongly accused. With embezzling you just never know."

Rachel's legs seemed to collapse. She sank to the floor and knelt there, clinging to the phone. Embezzling ... Abe? "No. Not Abe. He's so good and honest. I can see it in his eyes. He would never ..." Her throat seemed to close off. He did seem good and honest, but she could also sense he was insanely driven. A man didn't own a yacht like his and bring a crew of twelve to a vacation like this without being as wealthy as Joshua and Luke, who were both great guys but definitely workaholics and driven. They struggled to find a balance with work and family and would do almost anything to be successful. But her brothers had never embezzled or cheated someone. She pushed a hand to her forehead and tried to slow down her elevated breathing.

"There are quite a few articles about it," Luke said cautiously, not confirming or denying that Abe could never be an embezzler. "The initial ones show he'd embezzled from a company called McKnight Enterprises, apparently they're a big home security company. Shows Abe worked for them doing summer sales through college then they hired him after graduation. Less than six months later he was arrested for embezzling."

"Arrested!" Rachel shot back to her feet, the very word coursing fear and a fight or flight instinct through her veins. Arrested? Abe? She couldn't even fathom him in prison. It wasn't even possible. Was it? Had she been so taken by this handsome man professing she was beautiful even with her scars that she'd overlooked his deception? He was Preston's friend. Preston and that woman were obviously shady. Preston might be embezzling from Luke. Yet ... what if Abe was the one Preston and that woman were trying to steal from?

"Yeah. Three months in the Federal Correctional Facility in Cumberland, Maryland. It's a white-collar type prison, so not awful. He was initially given eighteen months to three years but was released after only three months when a woman named Angel Falslev disappeared with millions from the company and they determined that the original embezzlement was all on her and she'd set Abe up to take the fall."

"So he didn't do it? He was framed." She took a deep breath. It was okay. Abe wasn't a thief. Then why hadn't he told her he'd been in prison? They'd spent the past two days together, talked through a lot. He'd Googled her and knew all about her family, the bombing, and her scars. He should've told her. Prison was a big deal.

Luke didn't sound very sure when he said, "Probably not."

"Why are you thinking the worst of him?" Rachel all but shouted. Abe had been framed and she needed her brother to support her. She'd finally found the right man for her, a man who was so good he embraced even her deformed face; she needed Luke to support her and Abe. What she really needed was Luke to reassure her that Abe wasn't a thief, and of course he wasn't a liar, and he truly did love all of her.

"Well ..." Luke cleared his throat. "He and this Angel were engaged. And as soon as Abe got out of prison he started his own business and it skyrocketed quickly without any outside funding. Seems a little suspicious to me."

Rachel clung to the phone. She walked slowly to the couch and sank into it. Abe had been engaged? Had the woman framed him or was he in on it and he'd made it possible for Angel to escape with the money? Then after he was released, she shared it with him so he could start his business? Could they still be in contact? She pressed two fingers between her eyes trying to relieve the pressure forming there as her mind raced to even more awful possibilities. Abe hadn't fallen for her, didn't think she was smart, impressive, and beautiful even with her deformed face. He was in league with Preston and that blonde woman and was trying to use Rachel to trick Luke. No. Not Abe!

Despair coursed through her. Abe. She'd fallen so hard for him. Why couldn't he be perfect like she'd assumed? Why had she been so trusting and not checked him out right at first? She could've saved herself so much pain. Hadn't she had enough pain this past year? All her supposed faith crumpled and anger at not just Flint Brooks, but Abe as well, stirred her stomach until she was biting down the delicious dinner she and Abe had recently shared.

"You okay, sis?" Luke asked quietly.

"Yeah," she lied. "I'll hang up and read the articles." Her voice sounded as lifeless as she felt inside. It was a strange and uncomfortable combination—lifeless and in despair, yet so angry she wanted to go punch Abe in the gut.

"Are you going to confront him?"

"Of course I am."

"Do you think he'd get upset or violent with you?"

Rachel's eyes widened and she gasped. "No way! Not Abe. No!" Not even if she did punch him in the gut would Abe ever physically hurt her. Although, five minutes ago she hadn't thought he was capable of lying to her, of embezzling, of serving time, of being engaged to a woman who had stolen millions and disappeared. No. Abe could never hurt her. He'd been wrongly accused, right? Her head hurt as her mind spun a hundred different directions.

"Please be careful. Maybe wait until the morning when people are around or I can have one of the employees go with you."

"No way could I sleep with all this in my mind. I'm going to read the articles then I'm going to talk to him. He won't hurt me." No matter the questions running through her mind right now she could never believe that Abe who had so tenderly touched her scars and kissed her like she was his perfect match would hurt her. He hadn't tricked her into thinking he cared for her, right? Some people were exceptional actors. His sister was an actress. *No!* she screamed in her mind.

Luke blew out a breath. "Please be careful, Rach. I can't stand the thought of something happening to you."

He didn't say it but she knew he meant, something more. The bombing and recovery had been awful. At the moment, all that torture seemed to pale in comparison to Abe not being who she'd thought he was.

"Will you at least take your phone with you? Call Mar as you knock on his door and she and I will listen in. If we hear anything out of line I'll have some of the employees get there quick."

Rachel thought he was being silly, and she didn't really want anyone, even Mar and Luke, listening in to her conversation with Abe. It also felt like a violation of Abe's trust to have her brother listening in, ready to call someone if Abe hurt her. Was there a possibility Abe wasn't who he said he was at all and could actually physically harm her? No. No matter how confused and upset she was she truly couldn't believe that of him.

"I'll think about it. I trust him, Luke." Did she? Why was she itching to read every article about him and this Angel chick? Why didn't she just go to him now and let him tell her the story?

"Please be smart, Rach. Abe may have been planted on the island because you're there this week. Preston knew you were coming after all."

Rachel hated that as much as anything he'd said. Abe didn't really care for her? Had been part of Preston's plan all along? Her heart screamed no but her head argued that there was a grain of sense in Luke's reasoning.

"Mar and I will be praying for you" Luke continued, "And I'd really feel more comfortable if you'd call us before you go."

"Thanks, Luke. I'll be smart. Love you."

He heaved out a sigh, obviously realizing she would do what she was going to do. "Love you. Please at least keep your phone on you, even if you don't call us initially."

"Okay," she agreed. She hung up and paced for a few seconds. Should she go straight to Abe? Should she read everything and then confront him? Her stomach gnawed with worry and the sickening realization that Abe wasn't perfect. She knew no one was perfect and knew eventually she'd find out that he picked his teeth with his straw or didn't wipe down the sink after he shaved or something, but not something like this.

She let out a gargled scream and hurried into her bedroom. Changing into a comfortable short-sleeved floral romper that cinched at the waist, she dropped her phone into her pocket, downed a flavored water to help her dry throat, and pulled out her computer. Maybe it was wrong to not go directly to Abe, but she had to know what she was dealing with. He'd Googled her before they met and knew all about her accident. It wasn't really wrong to Google him and find out about his past. Or was it?

CHAPTER EIGHT

Abe couldn't sleep. The slashing rain and howling wind didn't help, but it was his constant thoughts of Rachel and the memories of her in his arms, their lips connecting that had him stirred up. He wanted to be with her and not have to say goodbye. Would it be wrong to walk over and simply ... hold her through the night? Protect her from the storm?

He'd changed into a t-shirt and comfortable cotton shorts, drank a bottle of water, and now paced his bungalow watching the storm grow in intensity. He'd spoken with each of his employees earlier and they were all doing fine. Would Rachel be afraid with the winds and the rain getting vicious? He'd closed all of his windows and the rain was now slamming against them.

He knelt down and said a prayer for Rachel and everyone on the island to be protected from the storm and then he checked in with all his employees again. They were all settled in their bungalows for the night. He knelt back down and said a prayer for Rachel to be protected from him. He knew if he went over to her bungalow his intentions would not be pure. He was far too attracted to her and wanted to kiss her and more, much more.

A pounding on his door startled him and he leapt to his feet. Rushing to the door, he flung it open and saw a drenched and very upset-looking Rachel. Her dark hair streamed around her beautiful face, her summery outfit clung to her appealing curves, but her blue eyes were stormier than the raging winds and slashing rain and her lips were pressed into a thin line.

"Are you okay?" He reached out and tugged her inside. She didn't come willingly.

"Don't manhandle me," she spat at him, tugging her arm free and stomping around him into the bungalow.

Abe's neck tightened. What had happened? How had he left his perfect woman with kisses twenty minutes ago and a spitfire with angry eyes had returned? She looked much more inclined to punch him in the gut than kiss him again.

He shut the door and turned to her. She folded her arms across her chest but her entire body trembled slightly. Abe didn't think she was cold despite being wet. The trembling was from anger and the look in her eyes was betrayal. He knew that look. He'd felt it when he learned what Angel had done to him. Angel. Betrayal. Prison. Thinking his life had been ruined.

Comprehension came quickly and his heart sunk. He should've told Rachel about prison, the events that led up to it, and all that had happened since, but it wasn't as if they'd had the time to talk through everything in their lives. She would understand they were still getting to know each other. Would Angel's betrayal never stop haunting him? If it ruined his relationship with Rachel, he might hire private investigators and hunt the woman down so she could serve prison time and he could finally have justice.

"You Googled me," he said simply.

She nodded, clenching her arms tighter around herself. "Actually, Luke Googled you and told me. I acted like the trusting dupe and thought there was no way my perfect Abe could be hiding anything from me." She gave a harsh laugh.

"Look." He held up his hands. He loved that she hadn't Googled him, that her brother had brought it to her attention. She'd trusted him, and with his issues that meant a lot. Now he needed to regain that trust. "I should've told you, I get that, going to prison is a big deal. But you have to admit that we've only had the past two days together. It's not the easiest thing to bring into a conversation."

She tilted her head and her long, dark hair spilled over her firm arm. The scarring on her skin glistened with wet rain on it. He loved every bit of her, including the scars. He thought she was incredible inside and out. Could they work through this? Would she forgive him hiding something ugly in his past? Angel. So perfect on the outside, so horrifically rotten and putrid on the inside.

"Did you read all of the articles?" he asked evenly.

She nodded. "Most of them."

"So you know I was set up and betrayed."

"By your fiancée. Some sources thought you were in league with her. You took the fall so she could get more money and then escape."

His jaw clenched, not only because of the unjust accusations but that she would lump him in with Angel. "But you wouldn't believe that."

She raised her shoulders, but her eyes told the truth. He'd

lost her trust because he hadn't shared. "I'm not sure what to believe," she said. "An innocent person would've come clean."

Abe tried not to react to that. "Ask me anything you want," he said quietly.

"Hmm." She harrumphed. "A little late for that, isn't it?"

A branch broke off a tree with a sound like a whip cracking and slammed into the window. Rachel jumped and it was all Abe could do to not rush to her and hold her close. He wanted to protect her and be there for her, but she definitely didn't look like she felt the same.

"Just a branch," he muttered.

"Yeah." She nodded and blew out a breath. "I do have a question for you though."

"Ask anything," he said, hope filling him. If she'd talk with him maybe they could work this out. He had nothing to hide, but if Rachel didn't trust him anymore he doubted there was any chance for a relationship between them. That thought sat heavy in his gut like one too many pieces of his grandma's pecan pie. He and Rachel's relationship had been more delicious than pie and he'd devoured it without abandon or thoughts of the consequences of not splaying all his dirty secrets to her. Now he was paying the price and it was heavy and made him feel sick to his stomach.

"Are you in league with Preston to cheat my brother?"

"Excuse me?" Abe was offended and confused now. Instead of talking things out she accused him of more. Abe would never cheat anyone and Preston would never cheat her brother. Preston was a stand-up employee and had been managing this island for years. Preston was an opportunist for sure but he wouldn't be so stupid as to risk embezzling from Luke Jewel.

"You heard me. Luke suspects Preston is embezzling from

the employee funds and has been for years. Nothing significant, not enough for anybody to notice, just enough to build up a nice off-shore account, and I overheard Preston and some blonde woman talking the first night I was here about taking money from somebody."

Some blonde woman? A sinister thought rolled through his mind, but Abe dismissed the idea offhand. No way would Preston be harboring Angel. No way. Yet, the two had been close friends. In college, Preston had fallen for her just like Abe had. Even though Preston had stepped back and let Abe and Angel be together, Abe had often caught Preston gazing longingly at her. That hadn't surprised him though, Preston had not only cared for her, Angel's looks had fit her name. If only her black heart had been a match for that sweet-looking face of hers.

"I don't know what you're talking about," Abe said. "I sincerely hope Preston isn't embezzling from your brother, he's always been a standup guy, but I can't answer for him. I will say that we have been friends since before college and I've never known him to lie or to not be a good employee." Preston suffered from the embezzlement just like Abe did, lost his job simply because of his association with Abe and Angel. It was all Angel's fault and the anger flared even hotter. Ten years later and still Angel was tormenting him. Now the duplicitous woman was messing up his relationship with Rachel.

Rachel simply glared at him. Abe pushed out a frustrated breath. Was there any way to get through to her? "Look I never embezzled from McKnight or anyone. If you read the articles you saw that I was framed by Angel Falslev." He winced as he said her name. "I spent three months in prison then was released when Angel fled the country with millions more of McKnight's money. The only thing you could say I've done wrong in the whole situation is the anger that's justifiably festered at the woman who set me up ten years ago. This is all Angel's fault, not mine and not Preston's."

Rachel pushed out a breath.

Abe took a step toward her. "Do you believe me, Rach? Can you give me a chance to explain it all, talk it all through?"

Rachel shrugged. "I don't know, Abe. I'm super confused about everything. I trusted you, I fell for you fast." Her voice lowered and she looked nothing like the Rachel he'd seen blossom over the past two days. She looked like an insecure teenage version of his beautiful, confident, sassy Rachel. "How do I know you weren't lying about us, about thinking I'm attractive, about how well you dealt with this?" She pointed to her left side. "You've got to admit it was a little too good to be true how easily you accepted me."

Abe's temper really flared then. He hated that she could think he might be an embezzler, but he could figure out how to deal with that. He could keep his cool when she accused him and Preston of tricking her brother, or of being in league with Angel, no matter how mad it made him. But he refused to stand here and listen to her disparage herself and think his attraction and feelings for her weren't genuine.

"Don't," he warned in a low growl.

"Don't what?" She flipped her wet hair and gave him a sassy glare with her blue eyes. The move actually reassured him. His Rachel was still in there.

"You can refuse to listen to my side about the embezzling charges and accuse me of anything you want regarding Angel or Preston. I can excuse that because you haven't known me long enough to know that I would never lie or cheat anyone, but I will not stand here and have you claim that what happened between us wasn't pure and meaningful. You ... are ... beautiful. Your scars don't detract from the picture that makes up Rachel Jewel, the strength, fire, and beauty that radiate from the inside and are reflected on the outside. You trusted me enough to show me your entire face tonight, to let me touch and be close to all of you."

He pushed a hand through the air in frustration before continuing from between gritted teeth. "Fling whatever accusations you want at me about my business or what happened with McKnight and Angel and I'll deal with that, but don't you *ever* pretend that I lied about how attracted I am to you. Don't you ever try to talk yourself into believing that I'm not head over heels in love with you because I *am*." The last sentence came out in a fierce snarl and his words honestly shocked him as much as they probably shocked her.

Rachel took a step back. Her eyes and mouth widened, and she tellingly put her hand to her left cheek. It seemed to take her half a minute to fully internalize his words, but then blue eyes glistening, she gave a little whimper and rushed at him. She knocked against his chest with her fists balled. Abe wrapped his arms around her and just held her there, using one hand to tenderly stroke her damp hair. Relief and joy swept over him. Rachel was in his arms. He could do anything with her close.

A sob seemed to rip from her as she slid her arms around his back and clung to him. She cried silently for a few minutes. Abe's neck and t-shirt were wet from her tears and her wet clothes seeping into his. He didn't like her crying, hoped he wasn't the cause of it, but he thought it was part of her healing and internalizing how much he cared.

Finally, she looked up at him and asked, "Did you *really* mean all of that?"

Abe studied her blue eyes and willed her to know he was genuine. "Every word," he said evenly.

Rachel gave him a tremulous smile and said, "I'm so sorry that I doubted you."

"Thank you." He kissed her forehead and said, "I never want you to have reason to doubt me again. Can we please talk through everything? Will you listen to my side?"

Rachel nodded. "I want to talk through everything. But first I want to ..." She ran her hands up the sides of his abdomen and over his chest muscles. His body reacted and he pulled her tighter against him. Rachel grinned and wrapped her arms around his neck, pulling his head down to meet hers.

She kissed him as if to show him exactly how much she cared. He'd admitted to her that he'd fallen in love with her. She hadn't said the same but her kiss seemed to say it.

A buzzing against his thigh startled him. Rachel didn't stop kissing him so he happily followed her lead as the storm raged outside. Another branch broke from a tree and hit something with a sharp crack as Rachel's phone buzzed yet again.

Rachel leaned back and smiled. "I promised Luke I'd answer his call."

He nodded solemnly, still a little upset with Luke for causing all the misunderstandings but he knew if the roles were reversed and it was his sister, Allison, he would do anything to protect her from someone who had a complicated past like his. At least Rachel was willing to talk it through, forgive him, and kiss him. He reserved any anger for the person it should be focused on—Angel.

She pulled her phone out to answer it, but stayed close to him, running her hand over his arm muscles, and making him want to kiss her all over again as she gave him a secretive smile.

A smile meant just for him. He wanted to be the man that Rachel smiled at like that. Always.

The rain pounded louder against the windows and he glanced out and saw the water in the swimming pool was sloshing as if it were on a cruise ship.

"Hey," Rachel greeted her brother. She smiled at Abe again. "Yes, I'm fine. I'm great, actually. Abe's great. We worked it out." She paused and listened. "Thanks, bro. A relief for sure. Yeah, Abe and I—" Her smile pulled into a frown. "Oh ... Okay. What do you need us to do?"

Abe's phone rang in his pocket. He wanted to know what Rachel's brother could be saying that had her frowning, but he thought whoever was calling at ten o'clock in the middle of a tropical storm might need an answer. Hopefully, his employees were all still safe inside. The speed and Wi-Fi connection on this island had impressed him when he dealt with work issues early this morning, but with this storm blowing in it was even more impressive that calls were still coming through.

The number said, American Express – Lisa. That was interesting. His personal concierge for his Centurion card didn't call often. "Lisa," he said in greeting.

"Mr. Bradford." Her voice sounded edgy, nervous. "Are you still at Paradise Retreat with your employees, sir?"

"Yes, I am."

"I'm sorry to bother you sir, but I felt this was worthy of your attention. I've been trying to reach the manager there, Mr. Preston Sant, but he has not responded to phone calls, texts, or emails."

As she said that he glanced at Rachel and heard her say, "Preston won't respond to you at all?"

He wondered how she'd overheard his conversation but realized she was still talking to her brother.

"What can I do to help?" He tried to ask pleasantly, but he wanted to know what Luke and Rachel were talking about. Anything with his credit card and charges with the resort could be resolved tomorrow. He had this exclusive card with no limit and a personal concierge so he didn't have to deal with crap like this. He paid the exorbitant yearly fee, spent millions on it per year, and had it automatically set to be paid in full every month. Why was she calling him when he wanted to be holding Rachel, and making sure Luke didn't sabotage him again?

"Well, sir. Initially, the charge came through several weeks ago for the Paradise Retreat for two-hundred and twenty-two thousand, eight-hundred and seven dollars."

"Yes, that was the cost of myself and twelve guests for the week."

"Well, in the past five minutes that charge has been repeated eleven times."

"Excuse me?" he tried to say calmly when he wanted to curse as he calculated quickly. Over two million dollars charged from this resort to his card? "Why wasn't it shut down?"

"It has been flagged and further charges stopped, but because your card is a no limit and you regularly spend large amounts, it wasn't stopped immediately. We're assuming it's just a glitch. The resort ran the charge repeatedly for some reason." Her voice didn't sound like she thought it was a glitch. "That's why we've been trying to contact the manager and resolve the issue. I realize it's only been a matter of minutes but I felt this needed attention and quick. Our system can often override such charges but we've tried, and the money is already gone." She paused for a breath. "I've gotten through to other staff members at the resort and they have repeatedly asserted they cannot refund the money without the manager's consent. I wanted to make you aware of the situation and reassure you we will remedy it, but if you happen to see Preston Sant, could you please have him call me immediately?"

"Oh, I'll find Preston Sant." His jaw clenched. What was his friend playing at? Where had he disappeared to? Was this really a glitch or could his longtime friend be cheating him like Rachel thought Preston was cheating her brother? The very idea turned his stomach. Even after ten years he hadn't forgiven Angel for her betrayal. Preston couldn't be doing the same.

Rachel looked at him, still on the phone with her brother. "Will you hold for just a moment, Lisa?"

"Of course, sir."

He pulled the phone away, ready to ask Rachel if he could talk to her brother and straighten out this credit card mess but then he remembered that Luke was the reason he almost lost Rachel, and her brother might be warning her to stay away from Abe at this very minute. So instead of accusing Luke's resort from stealing from him, he said, "Everything okay?"

Rachel shook her head. "Just a second, Luke." She pulled the phone away. "The storm is going to get worse. We're right in the path of a bad tropical storm, possibly a category one hurricane. The main body of the storm should pass over us around two a.m. Preston hasn't been responding to the weather service so they've been contacting Luke. Luke said the staff is going to gather everyone to the most secure spot, the spa and fitness center. Worst case we'll spend the night in the storm shelter. He's hoping we can help the assistant manager and other staff keep the group calm without Preston around."

"Of course." His stomach churned though. Preston had

disappeared, wasn't responding to calls? What was going on? Could his friend ... no he couldn't think it. Angel's betrayal still stung too much. If Preston had betrayed him he might lose the self-control he prided himself on. "I need to find Preston though. My credit card has been charged over two million dollars in the past few minutes from this resort."

Rachel's eyes widened and she got there quick. "You think Preston's stealing from you."

He wouldn't have outright accused his friend, especially not that fast. Could Preston truly steal from him? After all they'd been through?

Rachel stepped closer. "Abe. The conversation I heard with Preston and that woman. What if this is what they were talking about? They've taken money from Luke by embezzling from the employee funds, now they've hit your credit card repeatedly with the same charge so it took the credit card company a minute to catch up and now they're going to run with the money. It might be stupid to run during a storm but it would cover their tracks pretty well too. They might've thought it was worth the risk and since he hasn't responded to the weather service he might not know it's going to get worse."

Abe felt cold and a little lightheaded. Could Preston do that to him? "May I?" He opened his hand for her phone.

"Sure." She handed it over.

"Luke, this is Abe Bradford. The charge from your resort of over two-hundred and twenty thousand dollars has been repeated on my credit card eleven times in the last few minutes. Could a glitch like that happen?"

"No," Luke said shortly. "If a glitch like that happened, which it never should, it would happen immediately after the initial charge, not weeks later." He blew out an angry breath.

"I've suspected Preston Sant of skimming employee funds. I didn't want to accuse him without solid proof as he's been a fabulous manager and the former owner praised him, but now it looks like he's scammed you also. Well, your credit card company will get stuck with the charges unless they can recover them."

"We'll find Preston," Abe said with a clenched jaw. He didn't care if it was his money or the credit card company's funds, Preston wasn't getting away with it. The betrayal he'd felt when Angel had scammed him was horrific. He thought the wounds might heal now that he had Rachel, but he didn't know that he could live through that again. Preston. They'd been friends for years. *Please let it be a glitch.*

"Unless he's already skipped the island," Luke said.

"The charges were only made five or six minutes ago and it'd be suicide to leave the island in this storm." That said, the helicopter pad and then boat launch would be his first spots to look. Preston was a certified helicopter pilot.

"Good luck," Luke said. "Let me know when you find him."

"Thanks."

"Oh," Luke stopped him from hanging up. "Rachel seems to trust you implicitly."

Abe looked to Rachel, ecstatic to hear that. He trusted her implicitly as well and he never thought he'd feel that way again.

"Damage that trust," Luke's voice was full of warning, "and you'll have five angry brothers hunting you down."

Abe almost laughed, though the threat wasn't really funny. Despite Luke causing the mess earlier he thought he would like the guy. "Don't worry. My only plan is to increase that trust."

"Good. Stay in touch."

The phone went dead. Abe hurried to tell Lisa that he'd find

Preston Sant then hung up. A rap came on the door before he could talk to Rachel.

Abe pulled it open and one of the front desk employees stood there in a raincoat, taking a beating from the rain and wind. "Sir I need you and ..." He looked past him to Rachel. "Miss Jewel, there you are. I need you both to come with me to the main building."

"Miss Jewel will come with you; I need to find Preston."

The guy's mouth turned down. "Mr. Sant seems to have disappeared sir, he's not in his bungalow or his office."

"Are the helicopter and all the boats accounted for?"

"Yes, sir."

"Then he hasn't left the island yet. Call someone and get the keys out of the helicopter and any boats."

The employee complied quickly.

Abe thought of the blonde woman Rachel had caught a glimpse of. Preston could be hiding her somewhere. When the employee hung up Abe asked, "Are there any unused bungalows?"

"Yes, sir."

"Can you take me to them?"

The guy looked reluctant but he nodded. "There are raincoats in that closet."

Abe tugged open the door just off the entry, handed Rachel a raincoat, and put one on himself.

Abe turned to Rachel. "We'll take you to the main building then go find Preston."

She shook her head, her eyes determined. "No, I'm going with you to find that snake. He's stolen from my brother and you."

The employee's eyes widened at her declaration.

"I'd feel better if I knew you were safe," Abe said.

She put her hands on her hips. "I'd feel better if we stopped wasting time and found that loser."

Abe couldn't resist a quick kiss. "You're amazing," he whispered against her lips.

"I know," she said in response, yanking the hood of the raincoat up. "Let's go."

She took his hand and tugged him out the door. Abe pulled on his own hood and went willingly into the howling wind and slashing rain. No matter how his gut was churning contemplating Preston's betrayal, he was thrilled to have her by his side. He'd follow Rachel Jewel anywhere.

CHAPTER NINE

Rachel pushed through the storm; head bowed so the raincoat hood would keep her drier. Abe sheltered her with his arm but the pellets of rain stung even through the coat.

If Preston was the one responsible for stealing all that money from Abe, she couldn't imagine the betrayal he would feel. They'd been friends for a long time and just minutes before, Abe had vouched for him.

Her thoughts darted to Abe's sweet declaration to her. He'd said her strength, fire, and beauty radiated from the inside out. He'd said he'd fallen in love with her. It had shocked her how little he'd cared about the other accusations she'd made but wouldn't stand for her self-deprecating words. His words made her feel like she could fly and face anything, even judges or jury members staring at her scars and little children maybe being scared initially until they got to know her and she helped them know she would be their friend and representative. Maybe she could even forgive Flint Brooks and rid herself of that crippling anger. She felt like she could conquer the world and help the people she'd always wanted to help with Abe by her side.

She blinked up at him, the rain making it difficult to see clearly and the wind strong enough it was an immense effort to simply keep moving forward. Her hair was a mess, her makeup was gone, her scars were revealed, and she didn't care. All thanks to Abe. She loved this big, strong, impressive man. She hoped they could get through this mess and the storm and get back to kissing, talking about everything, and making more incredible memories together.

The employee who'd come for them, Kelton, gestured to a bungalow to their right, which had lights on. "This one's supposed to be unoccupied."

They'd checked out a couple other rooms, but they had been dark and nobody was there.

Kelton led the way and then they all huddled under the porch overhang. It wasn't complete shelter as the rain was slanting from the side but it was better than nothing. The employee typed in a code and tugged on the door. He frowned and tried the code again. The door still didn't open. He looked at them. "This is the universal code. It will override the code a guest puts in unless they're inside with the deadbolt turned."

Abe nodded and rapped on the door, yelling, "Preston, it's Abe."

A woman screamed in response. "No!"

Rachel's stomach pitched. Was the woman being hurt? Abe and Kelton looked at each other and both started banging on the door. "Let us in! We can help you!" Kelton yelled.

"Preston!" Abe hollered.

There was no response. Only the howling wind and the rain pounding against the roof and side of the bungalow. Abe looked to Kelton. "You stay here and keep knocking. I'll go around back and see if I can get in through the patio doors."

Kelton nodded and pounded again, calling, "Please let us in."

Abe squeezed Rachel's arm. "I'll be right back."

"I'm coming with you."

He didn't argue, simply wrapped his arm around her and they stayed close to the house, getting some shelter from the storm as they made their way through flower beds and bushes to the rear of the bungalow. Light spilled from the uncovered windows and glass patio doors. She could see Preston clearly and he had a blonde woman in his arms. The woman didn't look like she was fighting to be free, she looked like she was clinging to him, and sobbing. Rachel was pretty certain it was the woman she'd seen him with the first night she'd been on the island.

Abe's brow furrowed as he pushed at the door handle. It swung open and he ushered Rachel in with the rain as their companion. They both pushed their hoods off and wiped at their faces.

The woman spun around and Preston's head shot up. The woman's face was tear stained but absolutely exquisite. She was model gorgeous and Rachel recognized her immediately as the woman in the photos online with Abe. Angel Falslev.

"Angel?" Abe's voice was a low, disbelieving rumble. He clung to Rachel's hand as if she were his lifeline. She focused in on him and the anger and hurt in his face made her stomach roll. She wanted to comfort him and protect him from these two people hurting him ever again.

Kelton pounded on the door out front, but everybody ignored him.

"Abe!" Angel's voice was a lilting soprano, every bit as perfect as the rest of her. She yanked herself from Preston's arms and ran at Abe.

Abe's eyes widened in surprise as she threw her arms around his neck. Her hip bone hit hard into Rachel's stomach, pushing Rachel a few inches away from Abe. She gave Rachel a sweet smile and clung to Abe, as if she were meant for that spot.

Abe released Rachel's hand and she felt even sicker. He was going to fall for this woman, again. What man could resist a face like that? Truthfully, Rachel used to feel she had a face like that before the accident. A gorgeous face that turned heads and had men acting stupid. Not anymore. She fought the surge of jealousy. Abe had said so many sweet things to her. She clung to the belief that he did care deeply for her and wouldn't be taken in by a woman who'd betrayed him. Yet Angel was his first love ...

Abe took Angel's arms and pulled her away from him. He released her like she was a leper and stared at her as if she were an apparition.

Kelton knocked louder on the front door and yelled, "Let me in!"

"Abe." Angel's voice was pleading. "You look amazing. I can't tell you how I've missed you, how I've wished I could be with you all this time." She took a step closer.

Abe grunted in disbelief and sidestepped toward Rachel. He wrapped an arm around her. Rachel's heart leapt. She put her arm around his lower back and squeezed through the thin raincoat.

Ignoring Angel's pleading gaze, almost as if he would lose his self-control if he kept looking at her, Abe glared at Preston and said in a tight, barely-controlled voice, "You've been harboring her all these years?"

Preston spread his hands. "I love her, bro. I always have, always will."

Angel gave Preston a pitying look. "But I have always loved Abe. You knew that and tried to keep me from him. Even tonight, you're trying to make me leave during this horrific storm so Abe wouldn't find me."

Anger flashed across Preston's face but he schooled it quickly. "It's true, Abe. Don't blame Angel for any of this. She has always loved you and I've selfishly kept her to myself."

Angel brought her hands together as if praying to Abe and tilted her head so her long, blonde hair spilled across her full chest. "Abe ..." She stepped up close again and tried to stroke his arm. He yanked it away as if her fingers were acid. Her smooth brow furrowed but she persisted. "Abe, you have to know how much I've always loved you. Preston was behind all of it. He claimed they would put me in prison if I returned. He stole me away while you were in prison and has kept me on different remote islands so I couldn't contact you. Now you're here and you can rescue me like I've been praying for all these years."

Rachel held on tighter to Abe and said a silent prayer. Would he believe these lies? Could he see that Preston and Angel were toying with him? Angel was so sweet, so convincing. Rachel almost believed her.

"Don't!" Abe roared.

Rachel jumped but Abe kept her close to his side as he pointed one finger at Angel. "You have no clue how much I despise you." His voice was an angry snarl. "Don't you *dare*—"

The back door flung open again and Kelton walked in, slamming it behind him. He pushed off his hood, flinging rainwater everywhere. "I guess you got in," he directed at Abe.

Abe jerked his head to the side. "You wait on that couch. I'm sure I'll need your help in just a minute."

Kelton's eyebrows raised but he obeyed. Abe was a natural leader and obviously ticked off. Rachel didn't think even her tough brothers would disobey him at this point.

Abe looked back at Angel. His voice wasn't loud but it was piercing. Rachel could feel how taut his body was. It was as if he were exercising every ounce of self-control. "I will *not* listen to any more of your lies. You both betrayed me and you're both going to rot in prison." Anger dripped from his voice and Rachel would've been concerned for Preston and Angel if she didn't know how strong and in control Abe was.

Angel and Preston started talking over each other; interestingly, they were both trying to plead Angel's innocence. Rachel wondered if it couldn't be a plausible story. Preston could've kidnapped her, taken all the money, hidden her away all these years, maybe even tricked her initially and twisted the truth since. Yet, she'd heard that conversation between the two of them two nights ago and Angel had said something like she'd get the man they were going to steal from to fall for her. Abe. She would trick Abe.

"Stop!" Abe roared and Rachel jumped again.

The room fell deathly quiet. Only the rain and the wind broke the chilly silence. Abe took a few slow, heaving breaths and then he released Rachel and seemed to grow taller and more intimidating. Rachel was glad she was on his side.

"Preston, you are going to refund the money you just stole through my credit card." Abe's voice brooked no argument. It was a tone of *cross me and I'll cut your lying tongue out*.

Preston's face paled but he didn't move.

"Angel ..." He took another steadying breath, his dark eyes

full of righteous fury. "If you have any brain left in that twisted mind of yours, you'll stay far away from me." He gave her a look that said *don't you dare push me*. "As soon as the storm is over you will be returned to the United States and see exactly how miserable it is to pay for a white-collar crime. At least your sentence will be well deserved, and I'll do everything in my power to make sure you don't get off easy."

Angel whimpered and stared at Abe with red-rimmed eyes. Her look was pleading like a puppy dog who'd been wrongly punished by a cruel master.

"Don't," Abe warned, raising a hand. His anger radiated from him and Rachel didn't blame him. Being thrust into the path of the woman he'd long loathed for deceiving him and making him her scapegoat, and now having his close friend betray him as well. He was acting a lot more calm than she probably would have in his situation.

"Abe you have to believe me, you have to trust me," Angel begged. "He imprisoned me, tried to warp my mind, made me do … horrible things." Her full lower lip trembled violently and tears streamed down her face.

Rachel honestly wondered if she weren't innocent. She was so beautiful and sweet.

Abe completely ignored her. He walked to the laptop on the counter and flipped it open. "Password," he barked at Preston.

Preston's blue eyes were so malevolent Rachel wondered if he'd try to hurt Abe. Luckily, he didn't seem to have a weapon and he was much thinner than Abe, or Rachel was sure he'd be going after Abe. He didn't move though, simply whispered, "Angel1988."

"Fitting," Abe grunted with a voice full of disgust and

contempt. He typed it in. Rachel squinted and could see a banking account come up on the screen.

Preston was white and visibly trembling. "I thought you closed the window," he muttered at Angel.

She shot him a dark look.

"Unfortunately for you she didn't close the window," Abe said. She thought he might be relieved to get the money back but his jaw was rigid. His anger and betrayal obviously were much stronger than any worries about funds stolen. He started tapping away on the computer.

"What do you care?" Preston demanded. "The credit card company will take the hit, or the insurance company will. It was nothing personal and it won't affect you at all."

Abe gave him an incredulous look. His lips were tight and his jaw hard as flint. "I thought you were my friend, but all along you've been in league with *her* and now you try to steal over two million dollars and think I'm going to let you get away with it?"

"Come on. We've been friends a long time—"

"Exactly!" Abe roared. "That's what makes it so wrong!" His great shoulders heaved with emotion and he shook his head. "You were *never* my friend, and unless you want me to use your face for a punching bag I suggest you shut up and do what I say."

Rachel couldn't imagine how deep his anger at their deception ran. She wished she could help him somehow. He turned his back on Preston and finished tapping away. Finally, he glanced at Rachel and through his anger she saw a little of the softness he had for her. "The money's been transferred back from Preston's offshore account to the Paradise Retreat. Can you text Luke to transfer it back to my credit card?"

"For sure." She gave him what she hoped was an encouraging smile, pulled out her phone and texted Luke quick.

Abe shot a spiteful look at Preston. "There's only a few hundred thousand in this account now. Is this the money you embezzled from this resort or is it in another account?"

"No!" Preston yelled. "I earned that money."

"I don't think so. I'll transfer it back to the resort as well." Abe seemed to take pleasure in doing just that.

Preston clenched his fists, a vein popping in his neck, but he clamped his mouth shut as Abe had instructed earlier.

Rachel got a thumbs up back from her brother quick. "He's got it." She texted him that Abe had also recovered three hundred thousand he thought was stolen from his resort.

Abe pulled out his phone. He pushed a button and a second later said, "Lisa?" He turned his back to talk to her.

Rachel found her gaze drawn back to Angel. The woman was staring openly at Rachel's scars. Rachel instinctively grabbed her hair and pulled it around her face. Her neck burned, humiliated that she'd done that. Angel arched her delicate eyebrows, gave her a sympathetic smile, and then glanced away, as if she were as embarrassed for Rachel as Rachel was of herself.

She forced herself to shake her hair back from her face and stand straight and tall, but it felt like it was too late. Preston and Angel were both focused on Abe, as they should be. It wasn't like Rachel's scars or embarrassment mattered to the two of them.

Abe turned back and Rachel was secretly glad that he hadn't seen her reaction to Angel staring at her face. He nodded tightly at Rachel. "It's transferred back."

Preston's face looked ugly and terrifying but he smoothed it out quickly and splayed his hands. "No harm, no foul. Angel and I will just disappear. You can at least give us the dignity of not pressing charges, for an old friend."

Abe's dark eyes glinted dangerously. His fists clenching and unclenching. "There's plenty of harm and foul. You were *never* my friend."

"And we're not letting you disappear with the money you've been skimming from the employee funds," Rachel chimed in. "You wouldn't run with only two million and change. I'm sure Abe's credit card company stopped you taking all you wanted to but I'm also sure you've hidden millions more. Which account is the rest of the money in?"

Preston looked at her and arched an eyebrow. "You have no clue what you're talking about and I would think you'd want to be quiet and not risk that ugly face being splayed all over social media."

"Don't," Abe roared, finally seeming to break. He rushed across the space, grabbed Preston by the arms and shook him. "Don't you *ever* talk to Rachel like that."

Rachel's heart was racing, and it was all she could do to not pull her hair back in front of her face or run out of the room. The vicious storm was preferable to Preston and Angel looking at her like she was a lesser species. Preston with contempt and Angel with compassion.

Abe looked like he wanted to keep yelling, or possibly hit Preston. Rachel held up a hand. Even though Preston deserved to be pummeled, for so many reasons, she didn't want Abe to lose his self-control and regret it later.

"It's all right, Abe. This loser isn't worth getting upset over." They were brave words and she tossed her hair and tried to act as confident as she used to be. She might've been able to pull it off but instead of derision in Angel's eyes there was pity. Rachel looked away.

Abe stared at her for half a beat, then his shoulders relaxed and he gave her a grim smile. "You're right, Rach." He looked back to Preston and any semblance of a smile disappeared as he growled at him, "Where is the rest of the money you stole from the resort?"

"I don't know what you're talking about." Preston jutted out his chin, his dark eyes flashing.

Rachel was surprised at his bravery. He'd been Abe's friend a long time and knew how impressive Abe's self-control was. He must be banking on Abe not cracking completely.

Abe studied him then said, "You have no clue how much I want to beat the truth out of you, but I'm not a scumbag like you." His mouth pressed into a thin line. "I'll let the police get the truth out of you and I'll rest easy knowing you're both in prison."

Preston swallowed hard but wisely didn't respond.

Abe released one of Preston's arms but clamped his hand tight around the other and forcibly jerked the man toward the front door. "Kelton," he commanded. "You bring Angel." Kelton stood, his face glowing as if the prospect of holding on to Angel wasn't bad at all. "And please be advised that she is the devil, or on her very best day one of his minions. Don't fall for any of her tricks."

"Abe," Angel said in a soft voice. "Please. You have to believe I am innocent of all of this."

Again Abe simply ignored her. Rachel didn't know what to think. Angel could have been tricked or kidnapped. She truly looked angelic and she had only given Rachel sympathetic or kind looks. If she really wanted Abe, wouldn't she be glaring daggers at Rachel?

"Rach," Abe's voice was much gentler than it had been. "Can you please come on my other side?"

Rachel nodded, grateful he was still worrying about her and that he had stayed in control. Though Preston deserved it she didn't want to watch Abe hurt him. She walked to Abe.

"Where are we going?" Preston demanded. "You can't just take charge and make us your prisoners."

"Luke Jewel says I can," Abe said roughly, yanking on his hood on. "We'll wait out the storm with the rest of the staff and guests in the main building and then we'll get you turned over to the authorities." He dragged Preston to the door, unlocking the deadbolt and flinging it open. Rachel had gotten so used to the rain pelting the house she'd started ignoring it and almost forgotten how vicious the storm raging outside was. It howled into the open doorway, rain and wind stinging her through the raincoat. "Come closer, sweetheart," Abe said gently.

Rachel pulled on her own hood on and cuddled close to him. He shoved Preston out the door then he and Rachel went through. Abe wrapped an arm around her, sheltering her from the storm as best he could while dragging Preston along the path back to the main building. Angel and Kelton were close behind them, huddled together. Angel didn't appear to be giving him any grief, but Rachel couldn't imagine anyone wanting to fight much in this storm.

She was so confused about Angel and her seeming innocence. At least she wasn't confused about Abe. She cuddled into his side, loving his strength and his self-control. Most people would've at least taken a swing at Preston. Abe was singularly impressive and she was falling in love with him. She could hardly wait to get through tonight and be with Abe nonstop. She had no plans of leaving his side anytime soon.

CHAPTER TEN

Rachel stayed close to Abe, appreciating his strong arm and confidence as they hurried through the storm. The wind was at least at their backs, pushing them forward like an invisible hand. The rain slung at them from behind and from the side. It stung like a million tiny bee stings pricking against Rachel's bare legs. She cuddled deeper into Abe's side, grateful for his strong arm and large frame. He walked stoically forward as if the storm didn't bother him at all, sheltering Rachel and dragging Preston along.

Finally, she saw the large shape rise out of the darkness and the many lights of the main building appear up ahead. Unfortunately, the lobby was open-air. The beautiful flower arrangements were shredded—petals ripped and greenery strewn everywhere. The water features were still on and dancing wildly with the wind, many of them drenching the once-polished wood floors even more than the storm. The computer equipment behind the desks was most likely ruined.

They hurried through the main lobby and into the lobby of the spa and fitness center area. It was a relief to be out of the wet and the wind, but the air conditioning was running and almost immediately Rachel started shivering. Both the spa and all of the fitness center rooms were filled with people milling about. The fitness equipment that could be moved was pushed to one side. Employees were bringing guests warm robes from the spa, pillows, blankets, drinks, and food.

Abe looked to Kelton, who had his arm around a very wet Angel, nobody had offered her or Preston a raincoat. "Who's the assistant manager?" he asked.

Kelton glanced around and pointed. "Jason, sir."

"Jason," Abe called.

The dark-haired man was helping an elderly couple. His head darted up and his eyes widened in surprise as he took in Preston being manhandled by Abe. He excused himself and hurried to them. "Is everything all right, sir?" It seemed he didn't even know who he should address the question to.

"No," Abe and Preston said at the same time then glared at each other.

Rachel stepped forward. "Jason, I'm Rachel Jewel."

He smiled at her and to his credit his eyes only dipped to her scars and didn't linger there. "I know that, ma'am."

"Luke has instructed us to hold Preston Sant and Angel Falslev until the authorities can come for them after the storm. They have been embezzling from the company."

"You have no proof of that," Preston protested.

Abe silenced him with a look that would've quelled Jesse James. Preston tried to back away, but Abe held him fast.

Jason's eyes were wide but he schooled his expression quickly and nodded to her. "Of course, ma'am. Should we ... tie them up?"

Rachel looked to Abe. That seemed a little extreme and besides, where were they going to go in the storm?

"Did someone take the keys from the helicopter and the boats?" Abe asked.

Jason nodded.

"Then no. They have nowhere to go in this storm and they wouldn't dare run from me again." He gave Preston a significant look as wind and rain slammed into the windows.

"I don't know about Preston, but I won't run," Angel said sweetly, smiling at Jason. "I'm innocent and would be happy to prove that."

Abe grunted but didn't say anything to her. He looked to Preston. "You and Angel sit over in that corner and don't move unless Jason or Kelton escorts you to the restroom." It was not a suggestion at all but a command. *You obey or I'll rip you apart for what you've done to me* is what Rachel read between the lines.

Preston nodded shortly. Abe released his arm. Preston extended his hand to Angel. She tilted up her head and walked past him, turning back to give a parting shot to Abe with a beautiful smile. "Just think about how much I've always loved you, Abe, and what a snake Preston is. You know it's him who betrayed you, not me." She actually blew him a kiss.

Rachel would've thought it was comical if it wasn't done with the sweetest look. If she didn't know Abe's side of things and hadn't overheard Angel and Preston's conversation a few nights ago, she'd think this woman was as sweet as her younger sister, Eve. She felt jealousy roar in her gut. How could Abe stay impervious to her?

"Don't you dare speak to me again," Abe said in a low, cold voice that had several other guests staring at him apprehensively.

Angel's lips turned down, but she walked with Preston. They sat exactly where Abe had indicated, water dripping down both of their faces, but neither said anything to each other. Preston looked down at his clasped hands and Angel kept staring at Abe as if he were her hero.

Jason looked to Rachel. "What do you need, ma'am?"

"A towel would be wonderful, thank you."

He nodded. "And you, sir?"

They both tugged off their rain jackets. Jason automatically extended a hand and they handed over the wet plastic jackets.

"A towel and some water bottles, please," Abe said, then he turned slightly. "Kelton. Can you stay close to Angel and Preston, watch over them?"

"My pleasure."

Kelton scampered over to sink down close to Angel.

"Does Mr. Jewel want …" Jason didn't seem to know how to express it. "You in charge?" He looked between Rachel and Abe.

Rachel looked around, noticed the stacks of pillows and blankets waiting to be distributed and immediately went into action mode. "No, but I have a few suggestions."

He nodded, quick to please.

"I notice you have blankets and pillow ready. Please also have someone grab the yoga mats and distribute them and bring out any comfortable beds or mats from the therapy treatment rooms of the spa. I think it's important everyone stay together in this area. If the storm worsens we may need to move them quickly down to the storm shelter." He nodded his understanding. "Also, please crack the windows on the west side of the building to relieve the pressure of the windows being hit from the east. It keeps them from shattering."

Jason and Abe were both watching her with respect. "Okay. Anything else?"

"I'll let you know if I see anything." She smiled sweetly. "I know Luke will appreciate you being here for his guests through all of this."

His smile grew as if he realized the promotion he'd probably receive with Preston being suspended and most likely arrested for embezzlement. "Thank you, ma'am. I'll get those towels and water bottles and follow all your instructions. I apologize, but all of the robes from the spa have been handed out."

They both waved that off. Luckily, they weren't too wet and her summery outfit would dry quickly from her rushing through the storm to Abe's earlier without a raincoat.

"If you two need anything please let me know." He bustled off, still trying to hide his grin, and failing.

Abe arched an eyebrow at Rachel. "He's seeing a raise and promotion in his future."

Rachel nodded, wondering if Abe was really doing as well as he seemed. He'd raised his voice and almost hit Preston, but she couldn't blame him. He'd shown impressive self-control. She wanted to sit down and talk with him about it all. She glanced around at all the people and was surprised how many were staring openly at her and Abe. She wanted to cover up her scars, her hands twitched with the need. She held them steady.

Abe took her hand and led her over to a spot on the wall that was clear. Rachel could still hear the wind and the rain pummeling the building but she felt safe in here. It would be a long night with no luxurious bed or privacy but she felt like they would all be fine.

Jason came back with the towels, water bottles, and a couple of yoga mats for them to sit on. They thanked him and dried off their legs and her hair as best they could then they doubled the yoga mat underneath them and sat on them against the wall. Abe glanced over to where Preston and Angel sat with heads bent together, talking rapidly. He grunted and looked away.

"So ..." Rachel searched for the right thing to say. "How ya doing?" she asked it with a thick Jersey accent that used to make her brothers laugh.

Abe looked at her and chuckled. Rachel's eyes widened. "That was the response I was hoping for but not what I expected."

He sobered and passed his free hand over his face then shook his head. "What a nightmare, huh?"

"I can't imagine." She snuck a glance at Preston and Angel. They were both staring back at her.

Abe gave them a challenging glare and they both looked away quickly.

"I was surprised how ... convincing Angel's story was. Is there any chance she's innocent and was kidnapped by Preston?"

Abe glanced sharply at Rachel. "No chance at all." He shook his head and leaned back against the wall, closing his eyes briefly. "Angel is a master manipulator. She had me convinced that she loved me and then she set me up to take the fall as the embezzler, all the while embezzling more before she disappeared. I guess I should've realized she had help." He opened his eyes and Rachel hated the haunted, pained look there. "I never would've guessed it was Preston. I just assumed my closest friend was loyal to me like I've always been to him. Dumb, huh?"

"Not dumb at all and I'm so sorry."

He shrugged and studied his hands.

"So you think Angel has been here for the past, what was it, almost ten years?" She still was having a hard time wrapping her mind around that beautiful, sweet woman being a master manipulator and the person who framed Abe.

"It has been almost ten since she disappeared, but Preston's only managed here for the past four, I believe that's when this resort opened. Before that, he worked for other hotels and resorts throughout the Caribbean. I thought he simply liked the warmer weather and all this time they've been together. He's been sheltering her." He rolled his eyes. "Stupid sap that I am believing he was my friend."

"You aren't a stupid sap," she said, surprised that her confident, in charge of the world Abe was being so hard on himself. This betrayal ran deep. As it probably would for anyone. "You're a great person and it's not wrong to trust a lifelong friend, it's horrid of him to betray you."

"Thanks." He gave her a sad smile.

An employee approached them with a stack of blankets and a couple of pillows. "Do you want to try to rest?" the young woman asked. "They're going to dim the lights soon so everyone can get some sleep."

"Thank you."

Abe took the stack and they busied themselves spreading the blankets out and then laying down on top of the pile. It wasn't an awful makeshift bed with the yoga mats underneath. They both stretched out on the pillows and Abe said in a gravelly voice, "Can I hold you?"

"Yes," Rachel breathed out. He'd told her earlier that he was falling in love with her. She'd loved his impassioned speech about how the scars didn't detract from her beauty, but she felt like their relationship was tenuous. She wasn't sure if it was the whole deal with Preston and Angel or her insecurities lingering just below the surface, but something felt off and she wasn't sure how to fix it.

Abe slid his arm around her waist, and she rested her head against his chest, cuddling in close to his warmth and resting her hand on the ridged muscles of his abdomen. It felt amazing to have him hold her and she prayed that she was imagining the small rift between them. It was probably all between her ears, as her mom would say. Abe was amazing. He was dealing with something hard but he was still watching out for her.

The lights dimmed and the talking settled to a low hum. The rain and wind beat steadily against the windows. Abe's chest was firm and she liked cuddling up against him. Rachel found herself getting drowsier and drowsier.

Something startled her awake, who knew how much later, she thought it was maybe another branch thumping against the window. The room was even darker and very few people were stirring. Abe was breathing evenly, his body relaxed in sleep, his arm loosened around her. Rachel slowly sat up. Her arm felt the prickles sensation from being pinned between her and Abe's bodies. She needed to stretch and use the restroom. As she cautiously stood, Abe rolled over onto his side. She paused, but he didn't open his eyes and seemed to still be sleeping. Glancing down at him she was overwhelmed by how deeply she cared for him even though they'd only known each other for a few days. Would they have more time together after all of this passed? She felt like she'd be lost without him.

She shook her arm out and carefully made her way around makeshift beds toward the bathrooms that were located between the spa and the fitness center. She looked over to the spot where Preston and Angel were. They were lying close together with

Kelton not far away. That was good they hadn't tried to run. She looked at the windows and thought she could see the rain was still pummeling them, but it didn't seem like the storm was as loud. She was amazed all these guests staying at this high-dollar resort had been willing to listen and spend the night here rather than in their comfortable beds, but it had been a terrifying storm.

She made it to the lobby and looked out the huge windows. It was dark and scary looking still. Even though she thought the storm had calmed down she definitely wouldn't want to go back out in it.

She wandered into the ladies' restroom and used it and then splashed a lot of water on her face. Studying her face in the mirror, she was amazed at how good she felt. It was insane because her hair was a stringy, matted mess, she had no makeup on, and her scars were on display for anyone to see. Knowing that Abe thought she was beautiful had her feeling almost like her old, confident self.

The door opened behind her and she spun. Her eyes widened and she backed into the counter. Angel walked in slowly, blinking as if awakening from a deep sleep. She yawned and smiled at Rachel. "Kind of a miserable way to spend the night, eh?"

Rachel nodded, staring at the woman. She was other-worldly beautiful. Though she still looked damp and was probably uncomfortable, it was as if the rain and the long night hadn't affected her. It reminded Rachel of the Harry Potter books that her twin brothers Seth and Caleb had read nonstop, fancying themselves to be the Weasley twins. Angel was like Fleur Delacour, the part-veela, part-woman who was irresistible to the male species. Still, Abe was able to resist her, even when Angel had claimed her innocence and that she loved him.

"Excuse me," Rachel murmured, walking past her.

"Rachel," Angel's voice stopped her.

Rachel wanted to keep on walking but she didn't want to act like she was unable to face her boyfriend's former love. Boyfriend? Would Abe call himself her boyfriend? The thought made her smile.

Angel smiled at her, maybe thinking Rachel was smiling for her. "You've been through something really hard," Angel said, her eyes flicking to Rachel's scars. "I'm so sorry."

Rachel nodded, not wanting to talk about any of it with Angel. Before Rachel had been injured, she would've seen someone like herself and sympathized but never truly understood how it felt to be deformed. Angel had no clue how hard the past eight months had been.

"You're still beautiful." Angel gave her an encouraging smile. "I hope you remember that, no matter how the media or other people try to disparage you."

Rachel blinked at her. Her family were sometimes in the media but she'd been protected from it so far. The women at Harvard Law had mocked her but they hadn't known she was in that bathroom. Would people openly ridicule her?

"Abe is an amazing man. You're so lucky that he's fallen for you." Angel paused and seemed to debate then said softly, "You know Abe's already been through a lot with the media. I'm sorry to say but the two of you getting together will be a sensational story."

Rachel drew back. She'd gained so much confidence over the past few days, from Abe's acceptance and kindness and also realizing she was sick and tired of hiding away, it was completely contrary to her personality and the confidence her family and the good Lord above had always instilled in her. Yet … she couldn't help but glance in the mirrors and see the repulsive scarring. She touched the disfigured, bumpy skin on her chin and neck.

"You are a lovely person," Angel said sweetly. "I hope the media and others will see past the scars to the beauty you have within."

Rachel truly couldn't decide if the woman was an angel or a devil. She seemed so kind, so sweet, but Abe had said she was the devil and why would she try to plug these doubts in Rachel's head? Doubts of if Rachel was worthy of Abe and if she could handle the media pressure. She straightened her shoulders and smiled. She was a Jewel. She could handle it.

"Thank you for your concern. I'm sure I'll be just fine."

Angel smiled broader. "You go, girl," she said as if they were close friends.

Rachel returned her smile and pushed her way out of the bathroom. She made her way back to Abe and laid down next to him.

"Rachel," he murmured and laid his arm across her abdomen.

Rachel cuddled into his side and smiled to herself. She would be just fine. She could handle the media. She could handle disparaging comments. She was Rachel Jewel and she was ready to carve her spot in the world.

Abe's hand curled around her waist and she tenderly kissed his cheek before lying on his shoulder. She'd have Abe by her side as she figured out her spot. What else mattered?

CHAPTER ELEVEN

Abe awakened to pre-dawn light coming through the windows and Rachel cuddled into his side. He smiled and rubbed his hand along her lower back. She laid on her right side, facing him. Her dark hair was splayed across her left cheek and neck, semi-covering the scars, but not completely. He loved that she'd not only let him touch and see the scars, she'd also kept her hair back as they faced Preston and Angel and as they walked into this room full of people. She was amazing and tough, and he was completely smitten by her.

He realized the wind and rain weren't howling anymore. He glanced at the windows. It was a gray morning and the rain was still falling and many branches were broken and littering the ground, but the storm seemed to have settled. They were through the worst of it. Abe wouldn't have minded going and sleeping a couple more hours in his comfortable bed in the bungalow, but he wouldn't complain about holding Rachel close.

He did tilt his head up to make sure Preston and Angel were

still sleeping. With the storm tamping down he didn't want them to slip away. Maybe he and Jason should tie them up now. The thought gave him savage pleasure. He hated those two for betraying him. If they were arrested and he could have Rachel in his arms, maybe it would finally be the time to move past the anger and betrayal. He hoped.

He couldn't see them in the spot they'd been sleeping. Kelton was visible next to where they'd been. Abe's stomach gave an uncomfortable lurch. He gently disentangled himself from Rachel and sat up. His gaze darted around the room. He saw many people sleeping and some stirring but no Preston or Angel.

Then he heard it. The unmistakable chuff, chuff, chuff of rotating helicopter blades.

"No," he breathed out. He sprang to his feet.

"Abe?" Rachel asked, stirring in her sleep.

"I'll be right back," he managed.

Not bothering with his shoes, he darted around makeshift beds and out the lobby of the spa and fitness center. He ran through the rain-slick and messy floor of the lobby. The rain fell steadily but the worst of the storm had definitely passed. The noise of the helicopter drew him on. He cleared the lobby and through the trees beyond several bungalows he saw the helicopter rising in the air.

"Preston!" he hollered. He sprinted back through the lobby, past the pool area, and toward the beach. The helicopter slowly rose across the tree line. In the dusky pre-dawn Abe could make out Preston in the pilot seat and see the blonde of Angel's hair beside him. His former friend had been certified to fly a helicopter years ago. Abe remembered feeling proud of his friend's accomplishment. Had he hot-wired it or did he have a spare key the assistant manager didn't know about?

"Preston!" Abe yelled again. "No!"

Preston couldn't possibly have heard him, but he glanced down, saluted him with an almost sad-looking smile, and then he flew away. Abe wanted to sink into the sand in frustration and despair but he'd never been one to give up. He cursed himself for not tying those two up. They'd waited until the storm had calmed and found a way to escape.

His jaw clenched tight. He'd told Preston he wouldn't dare escape because he knew Abe would track him down. He hadn't had the resources to track Angel down ten years ago and then he'd tried to bury the anger and focus on growing his business. Now he was in a different spot. He could find them, and he would. He had the resources and the motivation. No longer would he be a victim to Preston or Angel. They both deserved to serve time and know how it felt. They deserved his wrath and much more.

With determined strides, he returned to the spa and fitness center. A few people were stirring but most slept on. Jason strode toward him. "Sir ... Mr. Sant and Ms. Falslev have disappeared."

"I know." He gave a sharp nod, his gut churning in anger, mostly at Preston and Angel but some at himself for not tying their miserable carcasses up. "They just took off in the helicopter."

Jason's eyes widened. "Is that safe in this storm?"

Abe shrugged. Maybe they'd crash and die and justice would be served. No, for all his anger he didn't want them dead, he wanted them in prison. "It's calmed significantly, but I'm going after them. I'll be taking my yacht." A yacht chasing a helicopter sounded impossible, but this pursuit wasn't about speed, it was about brains, money, and the need for vengeance. He had all three. "Will you watch over my people, and at the end of their stay return them to the airport in Belize if I can't get back?"

"Yes, sir. Anything else you need?"

Abe shook his head and glanced to where Rachel was still sleeping. Only Rachel. He needed her. He'd have to say goodbye, for now, but as soon as he caught up with Preston and Angel and got them arrested, he'd come for her. He walked slowly to her side, squatted down and touched her shoulder.

She stirred and blinked. Her beautiful blue eyes and incredibly appealing lips smiled up at him. "Hey, handsome."

Abe grinned back, amazed how one smile from her could wipe away all the anguish he was feeling. She was irresistible to him. How was he going to leave her? "Hey, beautiful."

She sat up and stretched and he had a hard time keeping his gaze on her face and not her beautiful body. "Breakfast?" she asked happily.

Abe chuckled at how cute she was but shook his head. "I have to go."

"What? Why?" Rachel scrambled to her feet. Abe straightened to face her. "You're leaving me?"

Abe's heart twisted. How to explain that he'd never willingly leave her but he had to track down Preston and Angel? He reached out and cupped her left cheek with his right hand. The bumpy skin didn't bother him at all. He loved that Rachel's beauty was unique and refreshing. "I don't want to leave you, but Preston and Angel escaped in the helicopter. I've got to track them down." He should never have underestimated either of them.

Her blue eyes looked sad and concerned. She reached up and put her hand over his. "Abe. Maybe you need to let them go."

"Let them go?" Abe stepped back and released her face. What was she saying?

"The anger and betrayal. Don't let it fester. I've done that with Flint Brooks, the man who hurt me. Let's forgive together. Let our hearts heal and move on with our lives. Please. Stay with me." She looked up at him so appealing he could hardly believe that he could walk away. Yet ... years of pain and betrayal. He'd always blamed Angel, but Preston was even more responsible. He hated them both equally now. What had been a festering splinter was now an oozing, septic wound. He had to catch them or he'd never heal.

"I'm sorry, Rach, but I can't let them go. They have to be arrested or I'll never have peace." He stepped back in, bowed low and kissed her tenderly. Straightening, he said, "I would never want to leave you, but I have to do this."

Rachel simply stared at him. He really wanted her approval, her understanding. Couldn't she see what they'd done to him? What they deserved? Several uncomfortable seconds passed with her searching his gaze but not saying anything. Then she wrapped her arms around his neck, pulled herself up onto tiptoes, and kissed him with a passion born of desperation. She didn't want him to leave and she loved him as much as he loved her.

Abe returned the kiss and knew that if she kept kissing him like this, he'd never be able to walk away. She abruptly yanked herself back, gazed at him with those brilliantly blue eyes, and said, "I love you, Abe."

Abe's heart soared. She loved him. What was he doing leaving her? But... Preston and Angel. The dark fury rolling through him at those two seemed to overshadow the love he felt for Rachel. "I love you," he said earnestly. Then he forced a smile and backed away. "I'll see you soon."

Rachel didn't reply, simply watched him steadily as he backed away and then forced himself to spin on his heel and jog from the room. He hated leaving her, hated letting the anger win over love. Yet he knew he had to hunt Preston and Angel down or he'd never have peace or be free to be with Rachel. He had no choice.

CHAPTER TWELVE

Rachel faced a long day on the island. The rain let up and she spent a lot of time walking through the beach and along the trails inland. When darkness fell, she ordered room service and forced herself to eat. The food was delicious but she had no appetite. She laid down in the comfortable bed. She should've been exhausted but she couldn't sleep. Abe had left. Maybe she didn't completely understand how it would feel to be betrayed by your best friend and your fiancée but she knew how it felt to be hurt by someone and need to forgive them. Flint Brooks had set the explosion that had ruined her face. She hadn't forgiven him and let it go, but she'd idealistically hoped she and Abe could work through that pain together. Maybe it would be easier for her as Flint was in prison and she knew he couldn't hurt anyone else. Maybe that was all Abe needed: Preston and Angel behind bars and not able to hurt anyone else, but she feared his revenge quest would hurt him more than it would heal. She prayed for her and Abe's hearts to heal and for protection for Abe in his pursuit.

The night slowly passed and the next morning she knew it was time for her to leave this beautiful island. She called the front desk for a boat ride back to Belize. She met with the manager, Jason, and felt he had everything under control. The staff had already cleaned up most of the mess the storm had created, and they all seemed happy and productive. She left a nice tip, hoping they'd soon recover the tip money Preston and Angel stole before they ran. In addition to whatever they'd stolen over the past four years from the employees.

She flew into Savannah, Georgia later that afternoon on a commercial flight. Luke, Joshua, or her dad would've all sent their jets if she'd asked but she hadn't wanted to wait.

Her mom and dad were both waiting for her outside the airport. They hugged her tight and her mom kept exclaiming. "Your hair! Oh, I love the way you're wearing it, sweetheart."

Rachel smiled her thanks, exhausted clear through. Her hair was tied back from her face and fell in long curls down her back. She knew her mom wasn't talking about her hair at all, but the fact that she was showing her scars and not hiding them. Even if she never saw Abe again at least he'd given her the confidence to show her face and believe she could still be attractive with the bumpy, uneven skin.

Her smile disappeared. Never saw Abe again. What kind of negative thinking was that? Abe would track down Preston and Angel, somewhere in this huge world, and then he'd come back for her. They loved each other. Of course he'd come back for her.

She walked with her parents out of the airport and climbed in their car. She told them all about the exquisite island and the fabulous experiences she'd had there, not telling them who she'd done them with, yet. When Abe came she'd introduce him to her parents and they'd immediately know how great he was and how the two of them were meant to be.

Her mom glanced over the seat at her. "And who did you have all these fun adventures with?"

Rachel looked into her mom's bright blue eyes. "Luke ratted me out?"

"No." Her mom shifted uncomfortably as if she didn't want to tell her. "Mar called. It's all over the media."

"Seriously? Luke's island is supposed to be paparazzi free."

Her mom nodded. "Luke was really upset. Apparently, an unknown guest took the pictures and sent them to *The Rising Star* and the article went viral. I'm sorry, love."

Rachel's stomach churned but she wasn't as upset as she would've been three days ago. She pulled out her phone and typed in her and Abe's names. There were some pictures of them on bikes, lying on the beach side by side, eating dinner outside Abe's bungalow, and even some of them in the main building during the storm. She laughed. "I look like a drowned rat in some of these."

Her mom's eyes were wide. "You're okay about this?"

Rachel shrugged and slid the article closed. She didn't love her face being splayed everywhere but it didn't look as bad as she'd feared, and Abe had looked amazing. She'd probably look at those pictures later simply to stare at him. She wondered briefly if Angel was the "unknown guest" who took the pictures but found she didn't care to know the truth. It would fit though as the woman had tried to make Rachel worried about the media "disparaging" her.

"It was bound to happen eventually," she said to her mom. "I met an amazing man on the island, Abe Bradford."

Her dad pulled into their tree-lined driveway and looked at her in the rearview mirror. "Amazing enough for you?"

"Just barely." She winked at him.

Her mom looked relieved and ecstatic. She loved welcoming new in-laws into the family and having married off all the boys happily, she wanted Rachel and Eve to find someone wonderful. She was probably even happier Rachel wasn't upset about her scars being displayed for the world to gawk at. It didn't matter. All that mattered was Abe coming back.

"And this Abe is the reason you're showing your beautiful face and not upset about those pictures online?"

Rachel nodded. "He helped me see that I'm brave, smart, and beautiful. The scars don't change that." As she said it, she realized that Abe had set her on her path to forgiving Flint Brooks. Yes, Flint had taken some flesh from her but she would come out stronger in the end and hating him would only hurt her.

"Oh, love." The car stopped and her mom jumped out and pulled open Rachel's door. She tugged on Rachel's hand. Rachel stood and hugged her tight. She got a little choked up, as if she were a child who needed her mom. She supposed she'd always need her mom. The hug was healing.

Her dad walked around the car and waited his turn and then he was holding her. He gently kissed her forehead. "If you think this boy is good enough for you, I might give my permission." His blue eyes twinkled.

Rachel laughed and blinked away the wetness behind her eyes. "Thanks, Dad. You'll love him."

"We'll see. When do we get to meet him?"

Rachel bit at her lip. "That might be a problem."

Her dad's brows drew together and she said another prayer that Abe would find Preston and Angel and come to her quick. She hoped it wasn't a vain repetition of a prayer that might never get answered.

Ten long weeks passed. June came and though it was beautiful in Georgia it was getting oppressively hot. Rachel got regular phone calls, FaceTime calls, and texts from Abe. He was always happy to talk to her and seemed like he was doing okay but neither he nor the high-dollar private investigators he'd hired had found Preston and Angel. They'd had some leads and all of them pointed to them still being in the Caribbean or possibly South America, but Rachel worried that Angel and Preston had caught wind they were being chased and would disappear for good. She begged Abe several times to come home and let the investigators look for them but he seemed to be more intent and obsessive with the search as time went on. His sister Allison had confided that his various assistants, team leaders, and managers were worried about his business profits sinking and wanted him home as well, but neither she nor the business he'd worked so hard for seemed to be the motivation to get him home. She had no clue how to get through to him.

She spent a lot of time talking with her parents and siblings about her future and finally shared the story with Eve about those two Harvard professors talking about her in the restroom. Eve had of course been outraged but Rachel reassured her that it was okay. It had been a setback, but she was going to rise above it.

She decided to go to law school and focus on family law. She'd received a score of 175 on the LSAT when she'd taken it last year, which was high enough to get into any law school she chose. She applied across the nation, flew to dozens of interviews, and got accepted to every school. The acceptance she was most interested in was the University of Buffalo. It was not a top school, but still in the top 100. Her parents and siblings were a little leery of her choosing a school based on the man she wanted to be with, especially since that man was still cruising the Caribbean and running his company remotely. Rachel had faith he was coming back. Someday. Every conversation he seemed a little more distracted and depressed, yet he always reaffirmed that he loved her and listened intently to everything she was doing.

He called late one night on an early June evening. Rachel took the call out back, walking the lush grounds of her parents' Savannah estate. The drooping Spanish moss on the evergreen live oaks was beautiful, almost shimmering in the light from the patios.

"Hey you." She smiled as she walked along the grass.

"Ah, just hearing your voice makes me happy."

Her smile grew. "I think if you saw me in person you'd be even happier."

He chuckled but it faded quickly. "You have no idea. How are you, beautiful?"

"Great. I got three more law school acceptances today."

"Well you're brilliant, and beautiful, of course they all want you."

"I don't think they care that I'm beautiful."

"Idiots."

Rachel laughed. She hadn't worn her hair in front of her face since she'd first styled it back for Abe. It was just another reason she loved him so much. He loved all of her. If only ...

"Any chance University of Buffalo is anywhere on your list?" His voice showed how much he doubted she'd even consider it.

"I had a great interview with them three weeks ago, and of course they immediately sent an acceptance letter for fall semester."

Abe let out a loud whoop that made her giggle. "You actually applied there and did the interview? Ah, Rach, you're amazing."

Rachel smiled but it slid away. "My parents and siblings think I should go to Cornell instead. It's only a few hours away from Buffalo."

"That'd be great too, Rach. I mean, I do have a private jet. It would make the commute short."

Rachel's smile returned. Though she knew it was completely impractical to fly to law school each day. "I suppose I could fly to you on the weekends."

"Not enough time," he said quickly.

"Says the man who's in the Caribbean with no plans to return soon." She should've felt guiltier for the quip.

"Ah, Rach. I'm sorry."

"No sign of them yet?"

"A few tips. Nothing solid."

"Come home Abe. Let this go. I'll go to the University of Buffalo. I just want to be with you."

Abe groaned. "It's not that easy, Rach."

"It is."

He said nothing and it was worse than him telling her off. "I'd better go. I'll call you tomorrow. Love you."

"Love you."

The phone disconnected and Rachel sank onto a patio chair.

How was she going to get through to him? They'd talked off and on about her going to him but she'd been busy visiting law schools and her siblings. Plus, Abe was busy and distracted, definitely not on some vacation, as he sailed to a different island every day and searched for any sightings or signs of Preston and Angel. Stubbornly, she wanted him to turn it over to his private investigators and let it go.

She stewed and prayed and then an idea she'd ignored and pushed away resurfaced. It would require her to not only show her face to the world and risk finding out if what those Harvard professors and Angel had said would be true. It would also require her to show that she could forgive like she was expecting Abe to do. She swallowed hard, said another prayer, and swept open her phone.

Searching her contacts, she pressed on Allison Bradford, Abe's little sister. They'd spoken on the phone a few times but hadn't met in person yet.

"Rachel," Allison greeted her in her deep, throaty voice. "How are you?"

"I'm doing all right. Not as fabulous as you though. Abe was telling me how proud he is of you landing a co-star role with Scarlett Lily."

"He's a good guy, that brother of mine and thank you, I'm thrilled with the role."

"I can't wait to see the movie."

"Thanks. I'll invite you and Abe to the premier. If we can get him home. What are your thoughts on that?"

Rachel swallowed hard and admitted, "I try every time we talk. Am I just being selfish? Does he need this closure?" Her family members agreed with her that he should leave it to the private investigators, but of course they'd agree with her, they were her family.

"Preston and Angel really did a number on him." Allison sighed. "But I don't like seeing the bitterness oozing from that handsome mug of his. He needs to let it go. He needs to be with you."

"Thank you. I ask him all the time. I hate being the nag, but I think he needs to let this anger go."

"From what Abe tells me you're the furthest thing from a nag. He adores you."

"Thanks." She paused then revealed the reason behind her call, "I have an idea. If I fly to California, would you do a short video with me to try to reach and help Abe? My siblings and I have some pretty great connections, add their reach to your social media, and we'll make sure it goes viral." The very thought of doing this video made cold sweat pop on the back of her neck but she wanted to help Abe. She'd do anything to help him overcome his anger and be whole again.

"Of course. What are you thinking?"

"Let's do a double-whammy. Spread the word about Preston and Angel and get them caught and show Abe exactly how much we both love him and need him to come home."

Allison didn't hesitate. "I'm in."

CHAPTER THIRTEEN

Abe used to be a big fan of the Caribbean, tropical islands, his yacht, the sea, and the sand. Not anymore. He just wanted to be back in the States holding Rachel close. Eleven long weeks without her. Half the time he wanted to just turn it all over to his private investigators and go home to her. The other half, he envisioned confronting Preston and Angel himself, pummeling his former friend and being completely impervious to his former fiancée. It was the closure and healing he needed. He thought.

He was combing a flea market in Ocho Rios, Jamaica. The shopkeepers were as aggressive as anybody he'd encountered in his travels. He bought numerous trinkets to appease them then showed them the pictures of Preston and Angel and hoped for information. Nobody had anything for him. Disappointment had been his constant companion on this voyage but he still tasted it like vinegar every time.

His phone rang. Allison.

"Hey, sis."

"Hey, you're going to be so proud of me. I'm part of a social media campaign that's gone absolutely viral. I'll send you the link."

"I'm always so proud of you."

She gave him a throaty laugh that he'd heard drove men insane. It made him insane to think of all the men who ogled and chased his sister. He always wondered who would be the lucky man to capture her.

"Thanks. Talk to you soon. Love you."

"Love you." He hung up and walked from the market. There was a beach not far away that wasn't crowded. He opened his messages and clicked on the video, drawing back in surprise when he realized it was not only Allison's gorgeous face but Rachel's as well on the screen. It hit him hard in the gut to see them together. His beloved sister and the woman he'd fallen in love with. He wanted to be with them. Hold them both tight.

They introduced themselves and he soaked up Rachel's tinkling laughter, bright smile and blue eyes. Her scars were covered with her hair, but it was still so wonderful to him that she was confident enough to do a video that had ... he squinted below their faces ... over six million views in less than a day. Would she be okay with that? He didn't know if Allison was doing a publicity stunt but quickly dismissed that idea as the two of them started talking about him and how he'd been framed by Angel and Preston. They showed pictures of both of the sneaky snakes and talked about a website where people could log information on sightings and help the investigators find the couple who'd not only tried to ruin Abe and McKnight Enterprises years ago, but also stolen millions over the past four years from hard-working employees on a Caribbean resort.

Then they changed tactics and Rachel shared about the explosion that damaged her left side and how she'd come to terms with her scars because of Abe's love. Then she said words that made warm chills surface on Abe's arms. "Flint Brooks hurt me physically and emotionally and for a while the bomb he planted made me feel like I wasn't worthy of happiness or success because my face had been disfigured." She slowly, deliberately pulled her hair back and revealed her cheek, chin, neck, and shoulder in a tank top style dress. "I'm asking Abe to forgive Preston Sant and Angel Falslev who both betrayed him. It's only fair I forgive the person who hurt me." She swallowed and said into the camera. "I forgive you Flint Brooks." The video paused on her beautiful face for a second and Abe felt warm and cold all over.

Rachel had forgiven the perpetrator. He could easily read that in her bright blue eyes. That hit him hard. She'd forgiven the man who hurt her. Could Abe forgive Preston and Angel like she was asking? She and Allison had asked him a dozen times or more to let it go and focus on his future with Rachel. He kept thinking in his mind that his betrayal was different because Angel and Preston had been his fiancé and his friend, respectively. Flint Brooks had been trying to hurt Rachel's brother Seth, not her. But was it really different?

"Life happens, Abe," Rachel said. "If we can forgive and let go of the pain it will be in our past. Yes, Preston and Angel took a lot from you. Don't let them take one more moment. Let's work together to let your anger go so you and I can have a future."

The video focused in on Allison and she shared a plea with the audience to please share the video and the website and to be on the lookout for Preston and Abe. Then the video zoomed in on Rachel again.

She smiled bravely and stared into the camera, but it was as if those blue eyes were focused on his soul, begging him to come to her. "Abe ..." His heart thumped faster. He loved her so much. "Everyone is going to help you find Preston and Angel. It's going to work out. Trust in the Lord and let it go. Come home to me. I love you."

The video zoomed back out and Allison repeated the information about the website and then it ended with the website link on the screen.

Abe clutched his phone. *Come home to me. I love you.* He loved her so much it hurt. Could he give up his dream of being the one to catch Preston and Angel? Allison and Rachel's website and viral video were great ideas and might be the thing that helped. People throughout the world would see the videos, turn in tips on the website. That was one thing that amazed him. No matter where he traveled, or how poor the people were, they had phones and Wi-Fi.

Maybe if he just gave the search another week or two. Abe could find Preston and Angel with the help from the website and video. It had received six million hits in less than a day, the video would definitely explode from there. Abe could be the one who caught them.

On the other hand, Rachel was asking him to come to her ... now. The need for revenge burned in his chest but he understood what Rachel was saying to him. He didn't want to give Preston and Angel one more moment and the need for Rachel competed with the anger he'd held onto for so long. He sank into the sand and muttered a prayer for help. He had no idea which direction to go.

Rachel paced the small cottage. It was on the waterfront of Lake Erie, about twelve miles from the Buffalo School of Law and four miles from Bradford International's downtown offices. The view was great, a green expanse of lawn and the endless waters of the lake. It might be chilly in the winter but that was okay. The bungalow itself was small, only two bedrooms, but it would be cozy. If only Abe would come and make it cozy with her.

She sighed, looking out the picture window at the lake. Abe. She and Allison had made the video trying to help him find Preston and Angel and asking him to come home four days ago and uploaded it three days ago. It had gone viral quickly and Allison had sent it to Abe two and a half days ago. Rachel hadn't heard from him since. She wanted to call but was forcing herself to wait on him.

She'd decided to go forward with her plans, find a place and get settled in Buffalo, get ready for school in August. If that didn't show Abe how committed she was to him she didn't know what would. Maybe she should fly to the Caribbean and sail around with him on his revenge quest until school started.

She heard footsteps and assumed the realtor had walked in behind her.

"I've fallen in love with this view," she said. "I like the whole place. I'll take it."

"I've fallen in love with you," a deep voice said.

Rachel whirled and gasped. "Abe?" She put a hand over her mouth, covering the whimper that leaked out. "Oh, Abe!"

He grinned and opened his arms. "You're taking the house; can I take you?"

Rachel rushed to him, wrapped her arms tight around his

neck, and kissed him hard on the mouth. He swept her off the ground and held her tight. "That depends. Where do you want to take me?" she asked.

He set her feet down and leaned back slightly. "I was thinking down a wedding aisle—a church, a Vegas chapel, a beach, the top of a mountain—wherever you want that aisle to be."

"Abe?" Her heart thumped fast and hard.

"Rach, I've been an idiot. I shouldn't have spent one day away from you." He looked more solemn, his dark eyes searching hers. "I let Angel and Preston take a lot from me, the three months in prison pale in comparison to the years I let the anger fester. I thought I was fine, building my business, acting like this successful, accomplished person but I wasn't fine … until I met you and you helped me learn to love, and forgive. Please forgive me for ever leaving you."

Rachel blinked fast but the tears still came. "You're here now," she said.

He smiled. "That I am. And I promise you I've buried my weapons of war deep in the ground."

"Your weapons of war?"

He nodded. "My anger and need for revenge. None of that is as important as being with you. Thank you for doing the video and helping me to see that."

"So the video was the ticket?"

"Seeing you and Allison together. Your plea at the end. It finally got through to me. I'm so sorry for letting Preston and Angel take more from me, time with you. I can't get back that time, but I want to do everything I can to be the man who's worthy of you."

"You're more than worthy of me." She kissed him softly but

it grew in need and the sheer amount of missing him she'd done made the kiss deep and desperate.

"Wow," Abe said against her lips. "Maybe I need to leave you more."

"Don't even think about it," she growled at him.

Abe laughed, released her, and dropped to one knee. He fished a round diamond solitaire out of his pocket and held it up to her. "Rachel Jewel, will you please do me the honor of being my wife?"

Rachel would've smiled at his formal lingo but her lower lip was trembling too hard. She dropped to her knees in front of him, snatched the ring and put it on her finger, and then kissed him.

She knocked him over onto his back and kept kissing him. Abe chuckled and held her close against him. "If I would've known this would be your reaction I never would've left you."

"Lesson learned. Never leave me."

"Lesson learned." He agreed and then he was kissing her again and they didn't need any lessons on that.

EPILOGUE

The huge chapel in Jackson Hole was filled to bursting. Rachel cracked the wooden door, peeked in, and saw all her handsome brothers lined up in the front next to Abe. Abe shifted nervously from foot to foot, his well-built body and handsome face showcased perfectly in a tailored tux. They'd gotten word days ago that Preston and Angel had been found in Brazil. They were currently being extradited to America to await trial. Abe had been strangely nonplussed, much more interested in he and Rachel's upcoming wedding. Oh, how she loved him.

"Somebody's anxious," Mar said from behind her.

"Get me married already," Rachel demanded.

Mar laughed. "Slow down, girlie. At least let Paisley and Krew walk down the aisle."

"Yeah, Aunt Rach, let me show off my pretty dress." Four-year old Paisley twirled in her pale blue dress, looking adorable as ever.

Krew shrugged, her new nephew was the cutest little man. "I just wanna eat cake."

Everybody laughed.

Rachel looked around at her sisters-in-law and sister. They all smiled at her in return. She was so blessed with wonderful people in her life. Her dad stood off to the side and offered his elbow. "Let's do this."

Rachel walked to his side, giving him a brief hug before linking their arms.

"All right." Mar spoke into her headset. She'd insisted on coordinating the wedding and had done an incredible job so far. Mar swung the door wide and the entire congregation seemed to turn. Rachel strained to see Abe over all the heads and was rewarded with a peek before Mar gestured her back.

Paisley skipped down the aisle, chucking her flowers at everybody. Luckily, most people laughed. Caleb's adorable little guy, Krew, followed, a few years older and much more serious as he held the rings on a satin pillow. Mar put her headset aside and strutted after Cosette, Breeze, Jade, and Emily down the aisle. Allison went next and then Eve and finally, finally it was Rachel's turn.

"You look beautiful, love," her dad murmured.

Rachel turned to him. Her veil covered her face, for now, but soon everyone would see her, all of her. Her white satin dress was strapless and fitted around the bodice then flowed softly around her legs with a long train. She knew Abe would love it. She had Abe to thank for the confidence to show her face, neck, and shoulder to the world, quite literally with how much attention her and Allison's video had gotten. "Thanks. Love you."

"Love you too."

Then the music changed to the wedding march and they

started forward. Everyone stood but luckily Abe was straight down the aisle and she could see him clearly, see the look of love and devotion in his eyes. When they reached him, and her dad placed her hand in Abe's, she felt the rightness of it clear through.

Abe leaned in close and whispered, "You're perfect to me, Rachel Jewel."

She squeezed his hand and said, "I know."

He chuckled.

The preacher raised an eyebrow at them. He proceeded with all the wedding words and she tried valiantly to pay attention but all she could think about was she and Abe. Together. They were finally together.

The preacher pronounced them man and wife and Abe lifted her veil. His gaze swept over her with appreciation and love. He gently kissed her. Rachel grinned and wrapped her arms tight around his neck, pulling herself up close to him. "Not good enough," she whispered against his lips and then she kissed him with wild abandon.

The audience clapped and hooted, but Rachel ignored them. She was with Abe. That was all that mattered to her.

Thank you for reading Rachel and Abe's story! If you enjoyed this fun romance, please keep reading for excerpts of more Jewel Family Romance.

Hugs,
Cami

Jewel Family Romance

Do Marry Your Billionaire Boss
Do Trust Your Special Ops Bodyguard
Do Date Your Handsome Rival
Do Rely on Your Protector
Do Kiss the Superstar
Do Tease the Charming Billionaire
Do Claim the Tempting Athlete
Do Depend on Your Keeper

DO CLAIM THE TEMPTING ATHLETE

Whirling, Eve found herself face to chest with a well-built man. "Oh, excuse me." She glanced up and the oxygen sucked from her lungs as she stared into perfection. The man had blue eyes that could rival the Jewel family eyes in brightness and clarity, a well-trimmed beard that complimented the strong planes of his face. He was smiling at her and the deep dimples in his cheeks, visible even through the facial hair, softened what would have been a face far too much like she'd always imagined Apollo would look like.

"Sorry I didn't see you," he said, holding his phone up. "Texting and walking."

"Should be illegal."

He slipped his phone into the pocket of his shorts and leaned even closer to her. "Eyes as pretty as yours should be illegal."

Eve's stomach hopped happily at the compliment but she forced herself to not fall into the trap of *his* beautiful eyes.

"Empty compliments will get you nowhere." She surprised herself by saying the line much too flirtatiously with a welcoming smile that clearly told him she wanted more empty compliments. Her sister, Rachel, and her sassy sisters-in-law would be very happy. They always gave her a hard time about never giving any handsome man a chance to flirt.

"It wasn't empty," he insisted. His gaze seemed sincere but what did she know? After her one failed attempt at a relationship she'd focused on getting through college in under three years while also being pregnant and having an infant and then toddler underfoot.

She lifted her eyebrows in an obvious challenge, compliments like that were always empty and were usually the prelude to an even more empty and meaningless dating fling. A single mom didn't have the time or energy for those kind of relationships.

She backed away then spun on her heel and headed toward the weight room. She heard him walking behind her but chose not to stop. She saw plenty of fit and handsome men in her gym and always stayed strong. Raising Paisley was her priority. She got lonely, but she had a great family to support her and interact with when she needed adult interaction.

She'd almost made it to the weight room when he touched her arm. Spinning, she folded her arms across her chest. "Can I help you?" she said it pleasantly, Eve rarely got snippety with anyone, but she didn't have time to flirt.

He nodded. She would've thought he was a very serious guy if his blue eyes hadn't been twinkling. With his tall, muscular frame, maybe six four or five to her five eight, and that mischievous glint in his eyes, he reminded her of her brother Caleb, about ready to play a prank or "sturdy trick" on someone.

"Yes, ma'am. I'm new to the gym and wondered if you could

show me around?" He glanced down at the fitted t-shirt she had all of her employees wear. The Fitness Spot emblazoned on her chest.

"Oh, shoot, I'd be honored to, but I have a personal training appointment at nine. I'll find someone else to give you the tour."

"Don't do that. I'll lift some weights while I wait for you."

"I have an appointment at ten also."

"Popular trainer."

She lifted her hands. What was she supposed to say? She tried to turn as many clients over to the other trainers as possible but many people insisted on her and then they told their friends about her.

"I'll lift until ten-forty five, shower, and meet you right here a few minutes after eleven."

"Do you always get what you want?" she asked. Partially annoyed he wouldn't take no for an answer and partially impressed at his tenacity.

"If it's something I really want." He shrugged and even though she was surrounded by muscular bodies every day she was impressed with the strength and definition in his shoulders.

"And a tour with me is what you really want?" She challenged.

"Yes, ma'am." His voice came out deeper and made her heart race faster.

Eve smiled at him and shook her head. "Fine. I'll see you right here a few minutes after eleven."

"Right here?" He pointed at his feet, his dimples growing deeper as he grinned at her.

"Not an inch to the left or the right," she shot back.

Keep reading here.

DO DATE YOUR HANDSOME RIVAL

Pushing her past away, Mar focused on the present, strutting down the aisle before the bride, her best friend. It wasn't truly a wedding aisle, just a stretch of sand on Destin Beach, Florida. Even though she was the master of five-inch heels, Mar had rarely tried to walk with them in sand while a wedding crowd watched her. It was murder. She sank all the way to her heel with each step and then had to yank said heel out and do it on the other side. She looked ahead of her. How had Eve and Rachel fared? They were already at the wedding arch, standing on the opposite side of their slew of handsome brothers, and their heels were probably only two-inchers. They were normal-sized girls who'd probably never felt the pressure to wear platform shoes to be taken seriously.

One of the brothers, Luke, stood out to Mar. He was perfection in a tailored suit. Not quite as tall or thick as Isaac, this brother was lean and mighty fine. He had golden-brown hair, a trimmed beard that had flecks of red in it, and the most gorgeous blue eyes she'd ever seen on a man. Other people might claim that the entire Jewel family shared the same blue eyes, but they obviously hadn't been caught in a staring war with this brother. Luke Jewel was ... delectable. His eyes were framed with dark brown lashes and lit with intelligence, grit, and an appreciation for her.

She almost tripped, but she recovered and kept plunging forward with a large smile enhancing her perfectly made-up face. Sweat was popping up on her brow, either from the way Luke's eyes lingered on her, or from the workout of walking up this aisle. Nevertheless, she tilted her head imperiously and kept working her way through the blasted sand.

If that look in Luke Jewel's eyes was sincere, she might grant the fine-looking man the privilege of entertaining her for the day. That was all a man could be for her, anyway: entertainment. She definitely had no inclination to delve into those blue eyes any deeper than that. She couldn't allow herself an involved manly distraction, not after failed relationship after failed relationship, most ending with the man explaining that she was too feisty and she ran when things got too hard. Well, duh! Look who'd brought her into this world: a mother and father who dumped their problems and ran.

She shook it off. She was busy running a highly successful perfume company, Cosette Industries. Her best friend was the genius who created all of their fabulous scents, and Mar was the one who marketed and grew the company. It had been a lot of hard work, an insane amount of hard, but maybe for today she'd let her hair down.

She finally made it to the front and sidled in next to Rachel and Eve. Turning with a large smile plastered on her face, she focused on her best friend walking down the aisle. She was ecstatic for Cosette and Isaac, and she would not succumb to her terror of being desperately alone like she'd been for years before meeting Cosette. She was Marietta Valez. No one and nothing would ever take her down.

———

Keep reading here.

DO TRUST YOUR SPECIAL OPS BODYGUARD

A low whistle from nearby didn't break Isaac's concentration on Cosette. He knew it was just Luke, finally taking a break from "discussing" with Dad—or, more likely, Mom had broken them apart and reminded them it was a party.

"Loony Lovegood's even prettier as an adult, isn't she?" Luke asked in a quiet tone, referring to the nickname Seth and Caleb had given her from their favorite books, the *Harry Potter* series. Seth and Caleb also fancied themselves to be Fred and George Weasley—magicians, tricksters, and inventors.

"Yes, sir," Isaac said, staring unashamedly at her. Instead of smiling in response, she narrowed her eyes and turned to her father.

"I'm not your commanding officer," Luke teased him. "'My best-looking bro' will suffice when you respond to me." He gestured to Cosette with his glass. "Beautiful, but what happened to her smile and sparkle?"

"That's what I've been wondering."

"You gonna go talk to her, or just stare at her all night?"

"How long have I been staring?" Isaac rubbed the condensation off his water glass and kept staring. Cosette darted glances at him, but whatever she and her father were talking about must've been very serious, as she never once smiled. Was Isaac not enough of a draw to command her attention? Could he bring her smile and sparkle back?

"Long enough," Luke said. "Dad noticed and sent me to tell you to be a man and make your move instead of just staring at her all night. He's afraid if you don't reveal your honorable intentions soon, he's going to lose his oldest friend when Blaine challenges you to a fight and you have to kill him with your bare hands." There was laughter in Luke's voice. He was the closest to Dad, but their father was their champion. He thought highly of Blaine, but he'd always said it was ridiculous that Blaine didn't think his boys were worthy of Cosette. If his boys weren't worthy, nobody was, Dad used to say.

"That would be unfortunate," Isaac said. "That was a direct quote from Dad?"

"Yeah."

"Does that mean I have his blessing to pursue her?" Isaac pulled his eyes from Cosette's beautiful face to look around the room for his father. He was busy talking to Heath and Hazel Strong, Stetson Strong, and Jade's sister, Teal, who he thought was dating or engaged to Stetson, a Texas Titans player who Isaac loved to cheer for. His dad caught his eye and gave him a wide grin and a thumbs-up.

"I think that answer is yes," Luke said.

Isaac felt hope blossom in his chest. Finally. He looked at

Cosette and found that she was focused on him again. She gave him a partial smile. Maybe it wasn't an invitation, but he was going to make it one.

———

Keep reading here.

ABOUT THE AUTHOR

Cami is a part-time author, part-time exercise consultant, part-time housekeeper, full-time wife, and overtime mother of four adorable boys. Sleep and relaxation are fond memories. She's never been happier.

Join Cami's VIP list to find out about special deals, giveaways and new releases and receive a free copy of *Rescued by Love: Park City Firefighter Romance* by clicking here.

cami@camichecketts.com
www.camichecketts.com

ALSO BY CAMI CHECKETTS

Jewel Family Romance

Do Marry Your Billionaire Boss

Do Trust Your Special Ops Bodyguard

Do Date Your Handsome Rival

Do Rely on Your Protector

Do Kiss the Superstar

Do Tease the Charming Billionaire

Do Claim the Tempting Athlete

Do Depend on Your Keeper

Strong Family Romance

Don't Date Your Brother's Best Friend

Her Loyal Protector

Don't Fall for a Fugitive

Her Hockey Superstar Fake Fiance

Don't Ditch a Detective

Don't Miss the Moment

Don't Love an Army Ranger

Don't Chase a Player

Don't Abandon the Superstar

Steele Family Romance

Her Dream Date Boss

The Stranded Patriot

The Committed Warrior

Extreme Devotion

Quinn Family Romance

The Devoted Groom

The Conflicted Warrior

The Gentle Patriot

The Tough Warrior

Her Too-Perfect Boss

Her Forbidden Bodyguard

Cami's Collections

Strong Family Romance Collection

Steele Family Collection

Hawk Brothers Collection

Quinn Family Collection

Cami's Georgia Patriots Collection

Cami's Military Collection

Billionaire Beach Romance Collection

Billionaire Bride Pact Collection

Billionaire Romance Sampler

Echo Ridge Romance Collection

Texas Titans Romance Collection

Snow Valley Collection

Christmas Romance Collection

Holiday Romance Collection

Extreme Sports Romance Collection

Georgia Patriots Romance

The Loyal Patriot

The Gentle Patriot

The Stranded Patriot

The Pursued Patriot

Jepson Brothers Romance

How to Design Love

How to Switch a Groom

How to Lose a Fiance

Billionaire Boss Romance

Her Dream Date Boss

Her Prince Charming Boss

Hawk Brothers Romance

The Determined Groom

The Stealth Warrior

Her Billionaire Boss Fake Fiance

Risking it All

Navy Seal Romance

The Protective Warrior

The Captivating Warrior

The Stealth Warrior

The Tough Warrior

Texas Titan Romance

The Fearless Groom

The Trustworthy Groom

The Beastly Groom

The Irresistible Groom

The Determined Groom

The Devoted Groom

Billionaire Beach Romance

Caribbean Rescue

Cozumel Escape

Cancun Getaway

Trusting the Billionaire

How to Kiss a Billionaire

Onboard for Love

Shadows in the Curtain

Billionaire Bride Pact Romance

The Resilient One

The Feisty One

The Independent One

The Protective One

The Faithful One

The Daring One

Park City Firefighter Romance

Rescued by Love

Reluctant Rescue

Stone Cold Sparks

Snowed-In for Christmas

Echo Ridge Romance

Christmas Makeover

Last of the Gentlemen

My Best Man's Wedding

Change of Plans

Counterfeit Date

Snow Valley

Full Court Devotion: Christmas in Snow Valley

A Touch of Love: Summer in Snow Valley

Running from the Cowboy: Spring in Snow Valley

Light in Your Eyes: Winter in Snow Valley

Romancing the Singer: Return to Snow Valley

Fighting for Love: Return to Snow Valley

Other Books by Cami

Seeking Mr. Debonair: Jane Austen Pact

Seeking Mr. Dependable: Jane Austen Pact

Saving Sycamore Bay

Oh, Come On, Be Faithful

Protect This

Blog This

Redeem This

The Broken Path

Dead Running

Dying to Run

Fourth of July

Love & Loss

Love & Lies

Made in United States
Cleveland, OH
15 February 2026

33433196R00095